W9-COI-027
Pb

THE COMPETITIVE EDGE

Schiller jumped to his feet, his eyes bulging. Reaching into his open locker, he whipped out a saber. Brandishing the gleaming blade, he said to Frank, "I'm going to give you a permanent souvenir of your stay here. You know what a Heidelberg scar is?" Schiller spun toward the others. "Hold him down."

Frank's adrenaline surged. He whipped around toward the other fencers, bracing for their attack. He knew he might fight off two or three, but against all six—including Schiller—his chances would be slim.

Then Frank saw the others hesitate.

"You idiots, I said grab him," Schiller shouted.

But the others hung back, exchanging glances. No one wanted to be the first to gang up on a teammate.

Schiller cocked his sword arm and screamed at Frank, "I'll make you pay for this!" Then he charged, swinging the big weapon recklessly.

YA
Dix
Pb

Books in THE HARDY BOYS CASEFILES™ Series

#1 DEAD ON TARGET
#2 EVIL, INC.
#3 CULT OF CRIME
#4 THE LAZARUS PLOT
#5 EDGE OF DESTRUCTION
#6 THE CROWNING TERROR
#7 DEATHGAME
#8 SEE NO EVIL
#9 THE GENIUS THIEVES
#12 PERFECT GETAWAY
#13 THE BORGIA DAGGER
#14 TOO MANY TRAITORS
#29 THICK AS THIEVES
#30 THE DEADLIEST DARE
#32 BLOOD MONEY
#33 COLLISION COURSE
#35 THE DEAD SEASON
#37 DANGER ZONE
#41 HIGHWAY ROBBERY
#42 THE LAST LAUGH
#44 CASTLE FEAR
#45 IN SELF-DEFENSE
#46 FOUL PLAY
#47 FLIGHT INTO DANGER
#48 ROCK 'N' REVENGE
#49 DIRTY DEEDS
#50 POWER PLAY
#52 UNCIVIL WAR
#53 WEB OF HORROR
#54 DEEP TROUBLE
#55 BEYOND THE LAW
#56 HEIGHT OF DANGER
#57 TERROR ON TRACK
#60 DEADFALL
#61 GRAVE DANGER
#62 FINAL GAMBIT
#63 COLD SWEAT
#64 ENDANGERED SPECIES
#65 NO MERCY
#66 THE PHOENIX EQUATION
#69 MAYHEM IN MOTION
#71 REAL HORROR
#73 BAD RAP
#74 ROAD PIRATES
#75 NO WAY OUT
#76 TAGGED FOR TERROR
#77 SURVIVAL RUN
#78 THE PACIFIC CONSPIRACY
#79 DANGER UNLIMITED
#80 DEAD OF NIGHT
#81 SHEER TERROR
#82 POISONED PARADISE
#83 TOXIC REVENGE
#84 FALSE ALARM
#85 WINNER TAKE ALL
#86 VIRTUAL VILLAINY
#87 DEAD MAN IN DEADWOOD
#88 INFERNO OF FEAR
#89 DARKNESS FALLS
#90 DEADLY ENGAGEMENT
#91 HOT WHEELS
#92 SABOTAGE AT SEA
#93 MISSION: MAYHEM
#94 A TASTE FOR TERROR
#95 ILLEGAL PROCEDURE
#96 AGAINST ALL ODDS
#97 PURE EVIL
#98 MURDER BY MAGIC
#99 FRAME-UP
#100 TRUE THRILLER
#101 PEAK OF DANGER
#102 WRONG SIDE OF THE LAW
#103 CAMPAIGN OF CRIME
#104 WILD WHEELS
#105 LAW OF THE JUNGLE
#106 SHOCK JOCK
#107 FAST BREAK
#108 BLOWN AWAY
#109 MOMENT OF TRUTH
#115 CAVE TRAP
#116 ACTING UP
#117 BLOOD SPORT

Available from ARCHWAY Paperbacks

CASEFILES™

NO. 117

BLOOD SPORT

FRANKLIN W. DIXON

Eau Claire District Library

AN ARCHWAY PAPERBACK
Published by POCKET BOOKS
New York London Toronto Sydney Tokyo Singapore

108985

Ingram 10/11/96 $3.99

The sale of this book without its cover is unauthorized. If you purchased this book without a cover, you should be aware that it was reported to the publisher as "unsold and destroyed." Neither the author nor the publisher has received payment for the sale of this "stripped book."

This book is a work of fiction. Names, characters, places and incidents are products of the author's imagination or are used fictitiously. Any resemblance to actual events or locales or persons, living or dead, is entirely coincidental.

AN ARCHWAY PAPERBACK *Original*

An Archway Paperback published by
POCKET BOOKS, a division of Simon & Schuster Inc.
1230 Avenue of the Americas, New York, NY 10020

Copyright © 1996 by Simon & Schuster Inc.
Produced by Mega-Books, Inc.

All rights reserved, including the right to reproduce this book or portions thereof in any form whatsoever. For information address Pocket Books, 1230 Avenue of the Americas, New York, NY 10020

ISBN: 0-671-56117-0

First Archway Paperback printing November 1996

10 9 8 7 6 5 4 3 2 1

THE HARDY BOYS, AN ARCHWAY PAPERBACK and colophon are registered trademarks of Simon & Schuster Inc.

THE HARDY BOYS CASEFILES is a trademark of Simon & Schuster Inc.

Cover photographs from "The Hardy Boys" Series © 1995 Nelvana Limited/Marathon Productions S.A. All rights reserved.

Logo design TM & © 1995 by Nelvana Limited. All rights reserved.

Printed in the U.S.A.

IL 6+

Chapter 1

IT WAS EARLY on a drizzly Thursday morning in Bayport, and Frank Hardy was in a hurry.

He pushed a slice of bread into the toaster, then waited for it to pop, holding out an umbrella like a sword. The instant the toast popped, he lunged forward with a shout of *"Et là"* and neatly speared the toast.

Frank's younger brother, Joe, appeared at the kitchen door. "Everything okay, Frank?" he asked.

"Fine," Frank said. "Just practicing my fencing moves."

"I don't get it," Joe said. "One day you're a normal, well-adjusted, eighteen-year-old American high school student who loves football and baseball, and the next, you're obsessed with fencing. What kind of sport is that?"

"Sport?" Frank said. "Fencing is not merely a sport. It's all about self-defense and chivalry and honor."

"Oh, please," Joe said.

"You should try it," Frank said. "It might improve your reflexes."

"All right," Joe said, grabbing another umbrella and pointing it at Frank. *"En garde,* you dirty scoundrel."

Joe lunged, aiming at Frank's chest, but Frank sidestepped and neatly knocked aside, or parried, the thrust. He gave Joe a solid crack with his elbow as Joe stumbled past.

Joe caught his balance, chuckled, and said, "Prepare to meet your doom, infidel."

"Give me a break," Frank said, cracking a smile and bracing his six-foot-one frame for an attack.

Joe whipped his umbrella at Frank's head in a terrific backhand slash. Frank nimbly ducked, and the umbrella swept past him, knocking a big pitcher of orange juice off the counter. The pitcher landed on the floor with a loud crack, and the juice splattered all over.

"Uh-oh," Joe said, just as their mother, Laura Hardy, appeared in the kitchen doorway.

"Joe Hardy!" she said. "Would you please act your age!"

"Sorry, Mom," Joe said, reaching for some paper towels to mop up the juice. "Frank was trying to give me a fencing lesson, and he got a little carried away."

"Sure, Joe," Frank said as he bent down and picked up the pieces of the broken pitcher. "If you had an ounce of my superior swordsmanship, we'd still have orange juice to wash down our toast."

"And maybe you'd have an umbrella stuck in the side of your head," Joe said.

After the brothers had cleaned up their mess, Frank checked his watch. It was already 8:07 A.M. They had thirteen minutes to make it to school. "We'd better get going," he said.

Laura Hardy picked up Frank's piece of toast from the counter. She turned it over to examine the hole in it and, shaking her head, handed it to him. Joe grabbed the other slice from the toaster, slung his book bag over his shoulder, and headed out the door.

"Sorry about the pitcher, Mom," he called over his shoulder. "I'll buy you a new one as soon as I can scrape together a few bucks."

Moments later Frank was backing their van out of the driveway after Joe slid into the passenger seat. "Step on it," Joe said. "I can't afford to be late for my English exam."

"Don't sweat it, you'll be fine," Frank said.

"You don't think Mom got too upset about the pitcher, do you?" Joe said.

"No," Frank said, "but we should go easy on her until Dad's back."

Their father, Fenton Hardy, an ex-detective who was now a top private investigator, was working on a case that had kept him out doing surveillance at night and home sleeping during the day for almost two weeks.

Joe spotted an extra-long, nylon navy gym bag between the seats. "I guess you're headed for the fencing club after school?"

"It's a *salle,*" Frank said. "If you're going to razz me about it, at least you could get the name right: Fencing studios are *salles.*"

"*Salle* . . . right—I feel so much better knowing that," Joe said. He rolled down the window and stared out at the passing scenery. "So what does *et là* mean, anyway?"

"It's French for 'and there.' You say it when you score a point."

"Sort of like saying 'take that,' " Joe said. "Not very sportsmanlike."

"Well, swordspeople have been saying it for centuries, so I'm not about to complain."

Frank had started classes at the Bayport Salle two months earlier, after taking a fencing class at school. When the coach said he had more natural ability than almost anyone he'd seen,

Frank gave outside classes a try. Now he was hooked.

"I still don't get it, Frank," Joe said. He knew a lot about sports—football, basketball, and baseball—but he was having a hard time understanding his brother's obsession with fencing.

"Look at it this way," Frank said. "Fencing's got the quickness of boxing, the timing of martial arts, the balance of gymnastics, and the one-on-one competition of wrestling. Add in chess-like strategizing, and it's the perfect blend of the physical and the mental."

"Mental—that's what I'd call it, especially those uniforms," Joe said as they turned into the high school parking lot. "Hey, could you drop me off? I've really got to get to that exam."

Frank pulled over, and Joe bailed. Crossing in front of the van, he poked the windshield with his finger five or six times, saying, *"Et là, et là, et là, et là . . ."*

After school Frank drove straight downtown and parked across the street from the Bayport Salle. Hurrying inside, he glanced at the gleaming gold fencing trophies lining the cases in the reception area, the tiny figures on top jabbing at imaginary enemies with needlesize swords.

In the men's dressing room, Frank changed into his fencing clothes: white knickers banded only at the knees to allow for quick leg movement, sneakers (leather shoes were only for official competitions), and a triple layer on top: a T-shirt, a protective one-armed padded plastron, and a heavy white canvas fencing jacket. After snatching up his white leather glove, which was padded across the back for extra protection; his over-the-head wire-mesh face mask with F. HARDY inked on the back; and his foil—eighty-eight centimeters of Belgian-forged, four-edged steel, with a circular-shaped hand-protector—he trotted out.

The *salle* had been used as a dance studio, which made it perfect for fencing. It was a large room with a high ceiling, a wooden floor, and one wall of mirrors so the fencers could watch themselves as they worked to perfect their form.

Thursday afternoon classes tended to be small; only a dozen or so die-hards were present. As always, they were a wide mix: young and old, men and women, big and small. Coach Kupcek liked to say fencing was a sport for everyone—the young had strength and endurance, but older students had tactics and finesse. Men and women fenced equally well. About the only thing they all shared—aside from a love of the sport—were superpowerful legs. Lunging, leaping, and bending for hours a day trimmed one's thighs and calves into solid muscle.

Frank had just begun doing his stretching exercises when he heard a familiar "Hi, Frank."

It was Juley Rouse, a strikingly pretty seventeen-year-old with short blond hair and light hazel eyes. If Frank hadn't been dating Callie Shaw, he definitely would have asked Juley out.

"Hey, Juley," Frank replied.

"Hey, yourself. Today Coach will name the team members to go to New York."

A month earlier, Coach Laslo Kupcek had told them about a major fencing tournament in New York City that weekend. Sponsored by billionaire businessman T. D. Brubaker, it would attract many world-class fencers. Because Kupcek's *salle* was small, it only rated three entries.

"I bet he asks you," Frank said.

"No way," Juley said. "I'm terrible."

"That's right," Frank teased. "Keep up your positive attitude."

Three sharp claps got their attention. Coach Kupcek stood at the head of the room. At sixty, he was short, thin, and balding, with bright blue eyes that danced behind his glasses when he watched a lively match. He had been a champion fencer in his native Hungary years earlier, and he was still quick with a blade, as he proved whenever he demonstrated technique to his classes.

Kupcek gave the word, and class began with

calisthenics to get the blood circulating, then moved to stretching exercises, especially for the legs and back. Ten minutes later, Kupcek said, "Fencers, take preparatory position."

It was the position of attention. Frank stood straight, heels touching, his left foot directly behind the right at a right angle, palms up and elbows straight. As everyone faced the mirror, Kupcek moved among them, making minor corrections.

"Good," he said, finally satisfied. "Next—*en garde.*" Quickly, Frank shifted position. Bending his knees outward, he balanced his weight evenly on both feet and brought his foil's tip level with an imaginary opponent's eye. Checking the mirror, he turned more diagonally to present a narrower target.

"I wish we'd start bouting already," muttered a voice behind Frank.

Frank glanced back. It was Adam Ross, complaining as usual. Tall, with black hair and blue eyes, he was the *salle*'s best fencer. He had started studying as a child in Washington, D.C., a major fencing center, then joined the Bayport Salle when his family moved there. The slim nineteen-year-old had talent and experience. Unfortunately, he was also a braggart.

"Patience, Adam," Juley whispered. "Even world champs have to warm up."

Ross scowled. Frank was impatient to get to

the bouts, too, but he understood the need for stretching and practice.

Fencers used three swords: the foil, the épée (pronounced EH-pay), and the saber, all slightly different and governed by slightly different scoring rules.

The foil, which all fencers learned on, had a flexible, lightweight, four-sided blade. The épée, slightly heavier, had a more rigid, three-sided blade, as did the saber, heaviest of all. The saber differed from the other two in an important way. With foil and épée the fencer could score only by thrusting. With the saber, the fencer could also score by slashing.

Bouts took place on a rectangular mat called a *piste,* or strip, about forty feet long and six feet wide. If a fencer stepped off the mat, he or she earned a penalty. Bouts ran to four minutes; the first fencer to touch the opponent five times was the winner.

"All right," Kupcek said, "prepare for bouts. Let me see some saber."

"About time," Ross muttered.

Frank wasn't surprised that Ross liked saber best—many experienced fencers did. With its thick, sharp-edged blade, it had a reputation for being dangerous.

"Saber's the Harley-Davidson of blades," Adam had once said. "You know why pirates used them? If you were boarding a ship, you could fight four guys at once. With a rapier, if you stabbed one guy, the others would get you. But with a saber, you could slash them all. The blade has a blood groove, so if you run someone through, suction won't hold it in. You just pull it out and keep stabbing and slashing."

Coach Kupcek eyed the group. "All right, how about Adam against Frank?"

Frank was surprised. He'd never fenced saber before. He looked across at his foe, who seemed to be even more shocked than he was.

"I don't know, Coach," Ross said. "He's a total beginner . . ."

The coach shot Ross a stern look. "And so were you once," Kupcek said. He turned to Frank. "I know you've never fenced saber before, Frank, but you've got the reflexes. The two of you should bring out the best in each other. Just one word of advice: Be unpredictable. Surprise him."

Frank nodded and pulled his glove tight. "Okay, let's do it." He reached for a saber. He'd only held one a few times and was impressed with its weight and also with the large protective bell that fit over the hand.

"Fencers, take your places," Coach Kupcek said.

"Good luck, Frank," Juley whispered.

Taking their positions on the strip, Frank and Ross faced each other standing at attention.

"And—salute," Kupcek said.

Cradling their masks in their free arms, the fencers extended their weapons toward each other, then flexed their sword arms to bring the guards to their lips, the blade tips pointing straight up. Then each briskly whipped his weapon toward his opponent again before donning his mask.

"On guard," the coach said.

Frank and Ross took the stance they'd practiced at the beginning of class.

"Ready," Kupcek said, "and . . . fence."

Immediately, Ross advanced and lunged. Frank parried, knocking his sword aside, then countered with an attack of his own, a riposte. But Ross parried in turn, then feinted, prompting Frank to defend high while Ross suddenly attacked low.

"*Et là,*" Ross shouted.

"Touch left," Kupcek ruled. Ross had scored a point.

The fencers resumed. Again, Ross came in, trying a similar move, but this time Frank was ready and parried.

"Very smooth, Frank," Kupcek said.

Ross's shoulders stiffened.

As they continued, Ross's greater experience began to show. He scored a second point, then a third. Frank was quick and his timing excellent, but Ross's years on the strip counted. He had a much bigger arsenal of moves and countermoves. Still, when Frank suddenly saw an opening, he lunged. The tip of his saber touched Ross's jacket near his rib cage.

"Touch right," Kupcek called.

Ross whipped off his mask. "He missed."

"He scored," Kupcek said firmly. "And Mr. Ross, mind your manners or you'll be disqualified."

Pulling on his mask again, Ross glared at Frank.

"On guard," Kupcek said. "Ready . . . fence."

Frank advanced; Ross lunged. Frank successfully parried and riposted, knocking his opponent's blade away to counterattack. Ross retreated out of range, then gathered himself, raised his saber overhead, and charged at full speed, his heavy blade aimed straight for Frank's chest.

Chapter 2

FRANK GRABBED ROSS'S WRIST with his free hand, yanked, and pivoted to the side in a perfectly executed judo move. Ross's blade sliced the air an inch from Frank's mask with a hissing sound. Ross flew past and stumbled to his knees, his sword clattering to the floor.

An instant of shocked silence filled the room. Then the other students burst into delighted laughter; a few even clapped their hands.

"Mr. Hardy." Coach Kupcek's voice cut through the commotion, silencing everyone immediately.

Frank whipped off his mask. "Hey, Coach, he went for my head. That's illegal, isn't it?"

"Maybe you don't remember," the coach

Eau Claire District Library

said, "but in saber any part of the body above the waist is fair."

Frank shook his head. "Sorry about that."

"It's okay," the coach said. "Anyway, your reflexes were good." The coach allowed himself a flicker of a smile. "When I said be unpredictable, that wasn't exactly what I had in mind. Needless to say, during an actual competition, you'd be disqualified."

"Hey, Adam," Frank said, turning to his fallen opponent. "Sorry." Frank bent to offer Ross his hand. Ross had removed his mask and was rubbing his knee.

"Listen," Frank said. "I saw the blade coming at my face, and I guess my reflexes kicked into auto pilot. You okay?"

Ross glared up at Frank, his lips tight. He looked ready to explode. Ignoring Frank's hand, he sprang to his feet, snatched up his sword, and pulled on his mask. "Let's finish this now," he said.

"No," Coach Kupcek said, stepping between the fencers with his hands raised. "That's enough for today."

"The bout's not over," Ross began.

"Adam, you're angry." Kupcek shook his head. "Don't make it a personal grudge. Better to have a rematch some other time. We wouldn't want anyone to get hurt, would we?"

With that, he turned to the group and signaled for everyone to line up.

"You've all been very patient," the coach began, once everyone was in place, "and I'm happy to announce the team we'll be sending to New York City this weekend. As I said last month, this tournament will attract many excellent fencers. Since we're a small school, we're allowed only three contestants, but I feel confident I have chosen the best to represent the *salle.* First, to compete in the advanced division—Adam Ross."

Ross nodded. Obviously, he had expected to be picked.

"And in the women's division," Kupcek went on, "Juley Rouse."

Standing beside Frank, Juley said, "Who, *me?"*

"Yes, you," Kupcek replied. "You're one of our best, Juley, and we have no place for false modesty in this *salle."*

Kupcek faced the group again. People shifted nervously.

"And for our final competitor," Kupcek went on, "to fence in the beginner's division—Frank Hardy."

"Thanks, Coach," Frank said. "I appreciate your vote of confidence."

"Now," Kupcek continued, "I assume you three can get out of school and attend?" They all nodded.

"Good," Kupcek said. "The tournament runs

tomorrow and Saturday. I've rented a van, so please be here at eight A.M. sharp. We'll arrive in New York by ten or so, check into the Collins Hotel, and you'll fence your first bouts tomorrow afternoon. And remember to bring proper shoes. If there are no questions, I'll see you tomorrow. And everyone else, wish your classmates luck. Maybe they'll bring home some trophies."

As soon as the Hardys sat down for dinner that night, Frank told them his news. All except his aunt Gertrude, who was out of town.

"Nice work, son," his dad said.

"I'm proud of you, honey," Laura Hardy added.

"A fencing tournament in New York?" Joe said. "Not bad. I haven't been to the city in a while."

"Why don't I ask Coach Kupcek if you can come, Joe?" Frank suggested. "I bet he wouldn't mind."

"Sure, I'm up for it," Joe said.

When Frank called Kupcek after dinner, he got the coach to agree as long as Joe covered his own expenses and didn't mind sharing a room with Frank and Adam Ross.

"Ross is kind of a jerk," Frank told Joe after he hung up. "But we won't be in the room that much."

The next morning, Frank and Joe arrived in front of the *salle* at a quarter to eight.

Minutes later, Coach Kupcek pulled up in a white van, and then Juley arrived carrying her bright red fencing bag. Her mother waved goodbye from their station wagon before driving off.

"Frank, would you mind driving?" Kupcek asked, holding out the keys. "I need to go over some paperwork on the drive."

"No problem," Frank said.

Eight o'clock arrived, then eight-ten and eight-fifteen, with no sign of Adam Ross. At eight-twenty, Coach Kupcek finally said, "I'm going upstairs to call his house." Just then a sleek black sports sedan cruised up. It parked, and Ross got out, yawning as if he'd just climbed out of bed.

"Everybody ready?" he asked, without a word of apology. He wore a navy blue blazer and sunglasses and carried a long black fencing bag.

Joe gave a little wink to his brother as if to say, You got it right. He's a jerk.

They all piled into the van and headed for the expressway. It didn't seem long before the Manhattan skyline loomed impressively before them.

"The Big Apple . . . just look at those skyscrapers, folks," came a voice from the backseat as they entered Manhattan. Ross, who had gone to sleep promptly upon climbing into the van, had woken up and was checking his watch.

"Weren't we supposed to be here a half hour ago?"

"We might have been if you hadn't been so late," Juley pointed out.

"Hey, don't blame me if Frank drives like a snail," Adam shot back.

"All right," Kupcek interrupted. "That's enough bickering. We're all here for the same reason, so at least try to act like teammates. You all know fencing teaches more than combat. It also teaches respect and courtesy. Something you should always bear in mind, Mr. Ross."

Listening to the coach, Frank recalled other fencing lore he'd learned in class—the history of the salute, for instance, a custom that dated to when knights who'd returned from crusades engraved their swords' pommels with replicas of holy relics they'd brought back. Before fighting, a knight would kiss the pommel to show respect. It was a custom fencers continued today, both before and after all lessons and bouts.

The Collins Hotel had a quaint air about it. Almost threadbare red carpeting covered the floor of the lobby, and the polished wood front desk had a gleaming silver bell to ring for service. Sparkling chandeliers hung above antique armchairs and plump-cushioned sofas with ornately carved legs.

The lobby was presided over by a watchful bell captain, who, with his constantly roving eye, seemed to notice every movement. He instantly whispered an order to one of his team of bellhops whenever anyone needed assistance. In his short red jacket, black bowtie, and white handlebar mustache, he seemed typecast to fit in with the Old World charm.

"This place is perfect for a fencing tournament," Frank observed.

"Hey, nice banner," Joe said.

Draped above the elevators hung a huge gold banner that read Welcome, Fencers.

"Okay, first we check in and take our bags up to our rooms," Coach Kupcek said. "Then we can come down and register for the tournament."

He stepped up to the counter to wait patiently for one of the busy clerks.

Frank, Joe, Juley, and Adam waited, too, casually glancing around the lobby where many people milled about carrying the familiar extra-long nylon sports bags.

Out of the corner of his eye, Frank noticed a man in a long dark coat moving quickly toward them. He was coming at their coach from his blind side. The stranger suddenly drew a saber from under his coat and shouted, "Kupcek!" as he flicked the sword through the air, the deadly tip aimed straight at the coach's throat.

Chapter 3

"WATCH OUT," FRANK SHOUTED.

Coach Kupcek tried to jerk his head back, but it was too late. The sword's glittering tip sliced to within an inch of his Adam's apple, neatly severing the top button of his shirt, which flipped into the air and bounced to the carpet. Before the mystery man could attack again, Frank lunged, seizing his sword arm. To Frank's surprise, the attacker was grinning.

"Kupcek!" the man exclaimed. "You're white as a sheet. I trust your students are better prepared to defend themselves against surprise attacks than you are."

Frank turned to Kupcek. "Coach, do you know this guy?"

Kupcek scowled. "Unfortunately, yes," he said. "Hans Hedrick. Still as showy and foolish as ever, I see."

Hedrick was of medium height, with close-cropped white hair. He appeared to be in his sixties, but a very trim and fit man.

"You can let go, young man," he said to Frank. "Your coach is safe now."

Frank released the man's arm.

"I heard you'd opened a small *salle,* Laslo," Hedrick said, then he addressed Frank and the others. "Your coach and I spent years on the circuit together. We crossed swords many times. He was always an easy target. Some things never change." He pointed at the carpet. "Now, don't lose your button, Laslo. See it down there?"

Kupcek frowned as he bent to retrieve it.

"I'm just sorry my team wasn't here to see the look on your face, Laslo," Hedrick said. He laughed, then turned back to the others. "Pleased to meet you all."

Frank, Joe, and Juley barely managed polite nods. But Adam Ross stepped forward, his hand out.

"Mr. Hedrick, the pleasure is mine," he said. "I've heard all about you, sir. You were quite the champion in your day, and it looks like you still are. I'm Adam Ross."

Hedrick smiled as he shook Adam's hand. "Ross . . . yes, I've heard your name. A promising young star, I understand. I hear you have a temper, too."

Ross seemed startled, but before he could say anything to defend himself, Hedrick held up his hands. "Now, don't make excuses—it's good to have passion. All the greatest fencers do."

"*Controlled* passion," Coach Kupcek interjected. "Passion without self-discipline is useless."

"Nonsense!" Hedrick exclaimed. He turned to Adam. "Take it from me, explosiveness is good. Be aggressive on the strip. It never hurt my career."

"Except for all those points you lost for poor sportsmanship," Kupcek said.

Hedrick waved his hand. "Most of the referees are in the dark—always have been, always will be." He turned again to Ross. "You know, you're probably like I was in my younger days. All you need is a coach who appreciates your style and can help you put it to work." Hedrick darted a look at Kupcek.

"Excuse us, Hans," Coach Kupcek said. "We have business to take care of here." And with that, he turned to the desk clerk and handed him a credit card.

"What did you think of Hedrick?" Joe asked. "Some character, huh?"

Joe and Frank were in the room they'd be sharing with Adam Ross. Joe stood at the bureau, unpacking his bag, while Frank sat on one of the room's two beds, checking his fencing jacket for rips or loose buttons. He knew how important it was to sew jacket tears and replace missing buttons immediately. Otherwise, an opponent's blade could catch in the opening. Ross, after tossing his bags into the closet near the front door, had left. Coach Kupcek and Juley were in their own rooms. The coach had told them all to meet downstairs in twenty minutes to register.

"Oh, he's a character, all right," Frank agreed. "That stunt with the sword was just plain crazy. If he'd been off even a quarter-inch . . ." Frank shook his head.

"Between the old show-off and the young guy with the attitude," Joe said, "I don't know about these fencers."

"Hold on," Frank said. "Coach Kupcek isn't a show-off—and Juley and I don't have attitude problems."

"But those other two more than make up for you," Joe said.

Frank glanced at his watch. "I should head down. It's almost one."

"I'm right with you," Joe said.

"Great," Frank said. "I'll take all the moral support I can get."

The fencing hall was actually a huge dining room with all the tables and chairs removed.

There were four fencing strips laid out and sections of bleachers for spectators on each side. At registration tables near the entrance, officials sat with computer printouts checking off contestants' names.

Frank and Joe met Coach Kupcek and the others for registration, then Frank consulted the match-up board. His first opponent would be Matt Novak, from Kissimmee, Florida, on Strip Three. Kupcek's three students weren't fencing at the same time, so they could all root for one another. As they made their way to Strip Three, the public address system boomed: "Ladies and gentlemen, before we start, we'd like you all to give a warm welcome to the man who has made this tournament possible . . . T. D. Brubaker."

A tall, dark-haired man about forty-five, wearing a perfectly tailored charcoal gray suit, appeared at the front of the room. "All I've got to say," he said into a hand mike, "is that fencing has given me so much pleasure. I'm sponsoring this tournament to give something back to the sport." Brubaker's steely gray eyes gleamed momentarily. "That's it—I'll keep this short so you can start. Thanks for coming, and good luck."

As the applause died down, Coach Kupcek said to his students, "Brubaker's a billionaire, the patron saint of fencing today. We should all be thanking him."

Kupcek's group joined the small crowd in the bleachers by the strip where Frank was scheduled first on foil. Frank had to admit he was a little nervous. The coach must have picked up on this, because he said, "Just concentrate on everything you've learned and practiced. Once the bout begins, you'll forget about all this noise."

Foil bouts were scored electronically because of the high-speed action. A tiny electrical switch in the sword's tip sensed valid touches and triggered the scoreboard automatically. Frank did well, winning 5–3 early in the third minute.

After Coach Kupcek, Joe, and Juley congratulated him, Frank was surprised when Ross offered his hand.

"Well done, Frank," he said. Ross grinned. "You didn't even have to use that judo move. Hey, sorry about getting so intense yesterday. When my adrenaline starts pumping, I guess I just turn into a wild man. No hard feelings?" He offered his hand.

Frank shook Ross's hand. "None at all—forget it."

Ross was scheduled next, fencing someone named Sheldon James on saber. Facing the fit, trim Ross, James looked particularly short and stocky.

After they had taken their positions and saluted, the referee barked, "Fence."

James started strong. He lunged and parried with impressive precision. But Ross fenced at least as well. Then, two minutes into the strenuous bout, James's footwork began to slow. His advances and retreats became less crisp. He was tired. Ross, on the other hand, seemed as fresh as ever, and it soon became obvious he was toying with his opponent. He would bait him to lunge, then parry and wait to score when he felt like it.

"Touch left," the referee called as Ross scored another point, his third point to none by James.

"They don't seem very evenly matched," Joe said.

"True," Frank said. "Usually they're closer in ability."

Then Frank noticed Hans Hedrick standing off to one side. The old fencing master seemed to be studying Ross carefully. During a break, Frank saw that Ross noticed Hedrick, too.

After that, Ross stopped toying and fought hard, striking his opponent's blade with punishing blows. Ross's aggressiveness was bordering on savagery. His opponent's vest and mask seemed to be meager protection against Ross's violence.

"Ross—yellow card," the referee said. Ross took the warning angrily, swiping at the air with his sword. The bout resumed, but just moments later, the referee yelled out again, "Ross—second warning: red card. Tone it down."

"Adam," Kupcek said. "Go easy, you've got this one won."

Ross ignored the warnings and kept stabbing and slashing viciously. Finally, while retreating from one especially powerful charge, James misstepped and stumbled. Ross just kept charging, though, and while James was down, he lunged, striking him in the chest.

"Ross," the referee's voice boomed. "Black card."

Ross spun toward the official. *"What?"*

"For excessive force and conduct unbecoming a competitor, you are hereby disqualified from this bout. You may leave the strip."

Ross whipped off his mask and stood his ground.

"Adam," Coach Kupcek said, stepping up to the strip.

"Mr. Ross," the referee repeated, "you will leave the strip."

"Come on, Adam," Coach Kupcek said. "Let's go, before you're disqualified from the whole tournament." Kupcek put his hand on the young man's shoulder.

Ross shook himself free. Turning to the referee, he said, "You're out of line, mister."

There were several murmurs from the crowd: "Send him home . . . Throw him out . . ."

But this only fueled the young fencer's temper. He wheeled toward the audience and shouted, "Anybody want to try?"

Then he stomped off the strip, snatching up his equipment and stalking out of the hall amid a buzzing from the crowd. After a few moments, Joe noticed Hans Hedrick following Ross out at a leisurely pace.

Coach Kupcek muttered, "I'd like to have a word with that brat, but Juley's up next. At least she won't take herself out of the bout."

Juley fenced well. Her opponent was good, but Juley was better, relying on techniques she had mastered at the *salle,* which included a devastating riposte. As she pulled off her mask after the bout, she wore an expression of joy and relief on her face.

"Very nice," Kupcek said, congratulating her afterward. Frank and Joe each gave her a high-five, and Juley beamed.

"I'm just going to call up to the room to see if Adam's there," Kupcek said. "I'll be right back."

Five minutes later, the coach strode back into the hall and joined the three teenagers, who were taking in another bout. "No answer up there," he said.

"Maybe he took a walk to cool off," Juley suggested.

"He could sure use it," Joe said.

They spent the next couple of hours watching a fascinating array of competitors and bouts at all levels of skill.

"Well, you're all off until tomorrow morning," the coach said as they left the hall around five o'clock. "I understand they have some activities scheduled for tonight. You should look into them. Registration's between eight-thirty and nine in the morning. Let's meet at the coffee shop at eight. Oh, and fellas," he said to the Hardys, "please let Adam know when you see him tonight. Right now, I'll try to find the referee and judges so I can apologize. We'll just chalk it up to stress. Adam was feeling the pressure and just blew up."

The brothers headed up to their room, which turned out to be empty.

"Where do you think he went?" Joe asked. "His overnight bag's still here."

"Beats me," Frank said, picking up the tournament timetable from the top of the bureau. "But remember when we first got here and he went off by himself? He probably did it again. Look, there's a screening of *The Three Musketeers* tonight. Want to go?"

"Sure. Why don't we invite Juley?"

Juley joined them for dinner and then the movie. The audience was mostly fencers, and everyone laughed during the sword-fighting scenes, yelling "point left" and "point right."

When they got back to their room that night, the brothers were surprised that Ross was still not there.

"Well, I'm turning in," Frank said around midnight. "I'm tired. I don't know how he's going to be able to fence tomorrow after so little sleep."

"Hey, Frank—Frank, wake up."

Frank felt himself being shaken. He opened his eyes and, rolling over in bed, saw Joe standing over him in the morning light.

"What's the matter?"

"Look at that," Joe said.

Joe was pointing at Ross's bed—perfectly made, its unwrinkled coverlet exactly as it had been the night before.

"Well, he obviously didn't sleep here," Frank said.

Joe went over and opened the closet where Ross had tossed his bags the day before.

"And guess what?" Joe said, showing Frank the empty closet. "No bags. Looks like he sneaked back in, took his stuff, and left while we were asleep."

"That's strange," Frank said. "I wonder where he went."

Chapter 4

"THERE'S NO WAY he'd miss his bouts today," Frank continued. "Fencing is this guy's life."

"Let's give Coach Kupcek a call," Joe said. "Maybe he knows something."

There was no answer in Kupcek's room, but, seeing it was seven-thirty, Frank said, "He's probably already down in the coffee shop. Let's go."

"Let me ask the front desk first," Joe said, dialing the operator. "Hello. Excuse me, but our roommate's not here, and we were a little concerned. By any chance, did he check out or leave his key last night?"

"One moment, sir, while I check," the clerk said. He came back on the line less than a minute later and said, "There are still keys out, sir, but I could ask the night staff and get back to you later."

"He'll probably turn up in the meantime," Joe said, "but thanks, I'd appreciate that." Joe hung up. "Okay, let's go hit the coffee shop."

Minutes later the Hardys crossed the lobby and went into the coffee shop, where fresh coffee was being poured and eggs and bacon were sizzling on the grill.

"Over there," Joe said, spotting Coach Kupcek's familiar gleaming pate and eyeglasses. He sat in a booth browsing through a newspaper.

"Hi, fellas," the coach said, looking up as the Hardys drew near. "Sleep all right?"

"Fine, Coach," Frank said, "but we're not so sure about Adam. He never used his bed, and this morning when we got up his bags were gone."

"How can that be?" he asked first one brother and then the other.

Just then a familiar voice sounded. "Morning, everybody." It was Juley. "Everyone's up before me, huh?"

"Juley," Frank asked, "have you seen Adam?"

"Adam? No, I just got up," she said. "Why, what's going on?"

"He never came back to the room last night,"

Joe said. "And this morning Frank and I found his bags gone."

"Wow," Juley said. "You mean he's, like, missing?"

Kupcek shook his head. "This is not good." He looked at the Hardys. "I guess I'd better call his parents."

"He'll probably show up at the registration desk between eight-thirty and nine," Frank said. "I'm sure he was just stewing over what happened yesterday."

"Do you think that's it?" Juley said.

"I don't see him passing up a chance to win the tournament unless something's really wrong," Frank said. "Let's just check the registration tables. For all we know, he'll have a reasonable explanation, and we can save his parents the anxiety."

After a quick breakfast, they all headed to the registration table in the fencing hall.

Once Frank and Juley had checked in and been given a list of their opponents and bout times, they joined Joe and Kupcek standing to one side. They stayed until the stream of registrants thinned to a trickle. Adam Ross never showed up.

"Where could he be?" Coach Kupcek asked as the registration table was shut down. "I hope nothing's happened to him."

"Well, we know he came back for his bags,"

Frank reminded the coach. "So we can assume he left of his own free will."

"Maybe he just went home," Juley said.

"Maybe," Joe said.

"I'm going to call his house," Kupcek said. "It's my fault. If I had kept a closer eye on him, he might never have left."

"Forget it, Coach, don't blame yourself," Juley said. "You know Adam. He doesn't listen to anybody but himself."

They all went into the lobby and waited while Kupcek used the pay phone. He had a brief conversation, and when he got off he hurried back to them and said, "The housekeeper says Adam's parents are on a cruise and won't be back until Tuesday. Adam didn't come home last night or this morning. I gave the housekeeper the number at the *salle.* I can call in for messages on the answering machine there. His parents are supposed to call me there. I suppose we should check with someone on the hotel staff."

"Done," Joe said. "Frank and I called down from our room."

"Then we should probably alert the police," Kupcek said.

"They won't take a missing-person report for twenty-four hours," Frank said.

"You seem very knowledgeable about this," Kupcek said.

"Our dad's a PI," Joe said. "We help him out on cases once in a while."

"Of course he is," Kupcek said. "With all this excitement, it slipped my mind. So what do you suggest, boys?"

"Go watch Juley fence, Coach," Frank said. "I'm not due on the strip till later, so Joe and I'll see what we can find."

The Hardys' first move was to head upstairs and leave a note on Adam's bed:

> Adam—See Coach Kupcek immediately. If he's not in his room, leave a message for him at the front desk and wait in the coffee shop.
>
> Frank and Joe

They gave a description of Ross to the hotel security chief and headed back to the fencing venue to ask around.

"My guess is Adam's disappearance has something to do with Hedrick," Joe said. "You saw how he was sucking up to Ross. And did you notice he left right after Ross stormed out yesterday?"

"Right," Frank said. "I wouldn't be surprised if Hedrick was whispering sweet nothings in Ross's ear about defecting to his team."

While they kept an eye out for the flamboyant ex-champion coach, they tried to get some information from a few other fencers in the crowd. No one was able to help, though.

"You mean that bad-tempered kid with the attitude problem?" the first woman they talked to asked. "No, I haven't seen him—and good riddance."

They got similar reactions from anyone else who had heard of Adam. He definitely hadn't won any fans at this tournament.

Several of Hedrick's fencers were warming up, but none of them had seen or heard from their coach since the night before, which they said wasn't unusual. He was known for his frequent comings and goings.

"I'll go check the room again," Joe said.

"Hedrick's first fencer is up soon," Frank said. "I'll check around quickly and meet you back here."

Frank circled the entire fencing hall, then he went over the coffee shop, the lobby, and the fencing master's room. No Hedrick. He met Joe back by the entrance to the hall.

"The note was exactly where we left it," Joe said. "I asked the maid if she saw anyone matching Adam's description, and she said no."

"I fence soon, and Hedrick's student should be fencing already," Frank said. "If he doesn't show up soon, then maybe they disappeared together."

"For a coach not to be there when his fencer's competing—isn't that weird?" Joe asked.

"Yep," Frank said.

It was only when Hedrick's second fencer began that the man finally appeared, strolling into the hall with an unconcerned look on his face.

Frank approached the veteran sword master. "Mr. Hedrick," he said. "We've been looking for you. By any chance, have you seen Adam today?"

"Ross? Not since his bout yesterday. Why?"

"What did you say to him when he stormed off the strip?"

"Not much," Hedrick said. "I said if I were his coach, I'd lodge a formal complaint against the referee. That sort of thing. After that, I was busy with my own fencers. Why do you ask?"

"He seems to be, well—missing," Frank said. "Would you let us know if you see him?"

"It's not my job to keep track of Kupcek's fencers, but, yes, if I see him, I'll tell him you're looking for him."

"Thanks," Frank said as Hedrick sauntered off to watch his fencer's bout.

"Why don't you get ready for your bout?" Joe said to Frank. "I'm going to check with the bell captain—you know, that old guy who seems to notice everything."

"Okay," Frank said. "See you back here."

Joe went out and down the hall to the lobby, where he cut straight across the red carpet to the bell station.

"May I help you, sir?" the bell captain said.

"I'm looking for my roommate," Joe said. "I think he might have left in the middle of the night."

"And what does he look like?"

"He's about my age," Joe said. "Tall, dark-haired, thin-to-athletic build . . . He may have been wearing a navy blue blazer."

The bell captain touched his finger to his mustache thoughtfully. "Well, I think I *did* see a young fella like that. Let's see—it would have been around two o'clock yesterday afternoon."

"You're sure about that?" Joe said.

"Absolutely. It's my business to notice everybody and everything in the lobby. He was standing right there." The bell captain pointed to a place near a large potted tree. "He was talking to another man."

"Another man?" Frank asked, surprised.

"An older gentleman. Thin . . . white hair . . . I think it was the same fellow who caused all the commotion with the sword in the lobby yesterday morning."

"Was it a long conversation?" Joe asked.

"Well, I'd say they spoke for at least five minutes."

"And you're sure about the time?" Joe said.

"No question. Every day after the movie matinee ends across the street, we get our afternoon coffee crowd. The lobby fills up, and I remember those two standing there, out of the way. Yes, I'm sure." Suddenly, the bell captain looked past Joe. There was an older woman waiting at the desk.

"Excuse me," the captain said, and left his station.

Joe went straight back to the hall and saw Frank stretching. He beckoned him over to a quiet spot in a corner of the room.

"It sure sounds like Ross was talking to Hans Hedrick," Joe said.

"Hedrick said he hadn't seen him since his bout yesterday," Frank said.

"The bell cap saw them huddling in the corner of the lobby for at least five minutes," Joe said. "Right around two o'clock, which was after Ross left the hall."

"In that case, I wouldn't be surprised if Adam resurfaces at the next tournament fencing for Hedrick's team," Frank said.

"Me neither," Joe said. "In the meantime, let's keep an eye on old Hans."

"I'm going to get suited up," Frank said. As Frank donned his jacket in a changing cubicle, Joe noticed Hans Hedrick taking a place next to the strip where Frank was scheduled to fence.

Was the rival fencing coach interested in recruiting Frank, too?

Moments later, Frank strode to the strip, gathering his mask and sword from the table nearby.

"Fencers, salute," barked the referee.

Frank and his opponent saluted, then pulled on their masks. All at once, Frank smelled something sweet coming from his mask. Had someone else been wearing it—Juley, perhaps? It smelled like perfume until Frank caught a slight whiff of a sharp, pungent odor underneath.

"On guard," the referee barked.

Frank looked at his opponent, a tall, powerfully built man named Johnson Drucker. Frank tried to concentrate, but the flowery smell was distracting him.

"Ready," the referee shouted.

Frank felt his chest tighten. There was a throbbing in his temples, and his jaw felt heavy.

"And—fence," the referee said.

Frank blinked. He tried to move his front foot forward, but it wouldn't budge. His épée suddenly felt as heavy as a sledgehammer.

What was wrong?

Frank tried to take another step, but the whole room began to tilt, and he staggered as his opponent charged.

Chapter 5

JOE REALIZED RIGHT AWAY that something was wrong with his brother. Frank had started out all right, but suddenly his shoulders dipped, his sword arm sagged, and the other fencer was on him.

Snatching a towel from a nearby chair, Joe whipped it toward the strip. It fluttered through the air like a football penalty flag and landed between the fencers. Frank's opponent hesitated as Frank collapsed to the strip, his épée falling from his hand.

"Stop the bout," called the referee, rushing forward and waving his arms. "Who threw that?"

The audience gasped as Joe ran to his fallen brother.

"Frank," Joe said, easing his brother's mask off and leaning close. Frank's head lolled, and his jaw hung slack. "Frank, can you hear me?"

Coach Kupcek came over and leaned in at Joe's elbow. "What's wrong with him? What happened?"

"Call a doctor," Joe said. He wadded a towel and placed it under Frank's head as he checked to make sure he was breathing.

"Coming through." Joe heard a woman's voice behind them. The next moment, a young woman in a white jacket with a stethoscope dangling around her neck and dark, shoulder-length hair, bent down beside Joe.

"I'm Doctor Falbo, the tournament physician," she said. "What happened?" Without waiting for a reply, she grasped Frank's wrist to check his pulse while delicately raising his eyelid with her thumb.

Frank mumbled.

"He just collapsed," Joe said. "I'm his brother."

"Does he have any medical conditions?" the doctor asked. "Epilepsy? Diabetes? Hypoglycemia?"

"He's in perfect health," Joe said.

"What about allergies—penicillin? Other antibiotics? Any food he's allergic to?"

Joe shook his head. "No allergies at all."

"Well, what about stress—has he ever fainted

"Go ahead and watch her bout, Coach," Frank said. "I'm fine here."

"Take it easy. I'll be back soon," Kupcek said.

"Frank," Joe said when the coach was out of earshot, "your mask was soaked with chloroform."

"I can't believe someone would go that far to make me lose. I mean, this is the beginners division—it isn't exactly the World Cup."

"Maybe they don't care if you win or lose," Joe said. "Maybe they found out we were asking about Adam Ross and they wanted to throw us off the trail."

"It's possible," Frank said. "So let's keep asking. Maybe we'll turn something up. Meanwhile, do you remember seeing anyone tampering with my mask—or even just hanging around?"

"No, do you?"

"No."

"Let's try the director, if you feel up to it," Joe suggested.

"Of course I do," Frank said.

They found him at a table marked Tournament Officials. He was wearing a badge that identified him as Alan Wyatt. The tournament director was short and round, looked to be in his fifties, and was surprisingly out of shape.

"No, the other floor pads never arrived," he said into a cellular phone while consulting a clipboard. "I *know* they were supposed to—ask Jim." He stabbed the disconnect button.

"Mr. Wyatt," Frank began.

"Guys, I've got fifty things going on at once."

"We just need a minute," Frank pressed. "We're looking for a fencer named Adam Ross."

"Did you try registration or the front desk?"

"We did. We think he might be . . . missing," Joe said.

"Well, if he misses his bout, he defaults—that's the rule," Wyatt said. "Now, you're going to have to catch me later."

The director turned and started to dial another number.

"Frank," Joe said under his breath. "Isn't that the big cheese coming this way?"

Turning, Frank saw T. D. Brubaker striding toward the table. Wyatt saw him, too, and he immediately hung up the phone. "Mr. Brubaker," he said. "Hello, sir."

"Everything all right, Wyatt?" Brubaker asked.

Standing close, Joe could sense the billionaire's no-nonsense attitude. He was impeccably groomed. This and the firm set of his jaw served to accentuate a small scar across his right cheekbone.

"Oh, great, sir," Wyatt said. "Just a few small snags, but nothing we can't handle. Can I show you the matting that came? It's not what we ordered, but we can probably use it anyway."

"You lead the way," Brubaker said.

"Sir?" Frank said, trying to talk to the billionaire.

"Sorry, guys," Wyatt said, quickly stepping in front of the Hardys. "We have a tournament to run here. Now, if you'll please excuse us." And with that, he led the sponsor away.

"What about that group over there?" Joe asked.

There was a small crowd of white-clad fencers standing around a nearby refreshment table, munching doughnuts and sipping coffee.

"Let's give them a try," Frank said.

Hearing of Ross's disappearance, one tall, fiftyish man said, "Dropped out, did he? Well, these days it'd be an unusual tournament if someone didn't—"

"Excuse me?" Frank said.

"I mean, there have been other cases like this. Bob Gale a few months ago in Chicago, and Carlos DeMarco in Philly."

"And Frank Fontano," a short younger man added.

"Fontano didn't drop out," corrected a red-haired woman. "He got hurt skydiving. I hear he's going to be okay, though."

"Well, there are still the others," the short

man said. "Brett Stanton, too, come to think of it."

"Brett Stanton—you're right. We *have* had a lot of dropouts lately." The man turned to the Hardys. "Not that it's surprising, especially the newcomers. They fall in love with the sport, then when they realize there's no money in it, they drift away."

"There's no money because there are no audiences," the woman said. "Fencing's a bad spectator sport. You can't watch it in a stadium, or even on TV; the action's too quick, and the rules are too complicated. Most people wouldn't have any idea how to follow it."

"We have had a lot of dropouts," an older woman said. "Sometimes I think the younger people these days just don't have the patience to stick with a sport that takes so much practice."

After a few more minutes of the same, the Hardys thanked the fencers and excused themselves. They went back over to join Coach Kupcek and Juley, who had lost a close bout in the semifinals of the junior women's division—a very respectable showing in her first tournament.

"Well, it's about time to leave," the coach said. "Why don't you three go collect your bags, and we'll meet in the lobby in half an hour?"

* * *

The drive back was quiet, Ross's absence having left a very conspicuous space in the back of the van. When they pulled up to the *salle,* they found Juley's mother waiting. Frank and Joe congratulated Juley one more time on her showing, and she gave them a halfhearted wave as the station wagon drove away.

"I'll call you two if I hear anything," Coach Kupcek said, "and I trust you'll do the same."

"Count on us being in touch soon," Frank said.

A short while later, as Frank pulled their van into the Hardys' driveway, he said to Joe, "There's nothing more for us to do about finding Ross tonight. I'm heading over to Callie's to see if she wants to go grab a pizza. Vanessa is busy, right?"

Joe nodded. His girlfriend, Vanessa Bender, was working on an animation project with her mom all weekend and had left strict orders not to be disturbed.

"Could you let Mom and Dad know?" Frank asked.

Later that night Frank drove home, still puzzling about Adam Ross. He had told Callie all about the situation over a large pie with the works at Mr. Pizza and had decided there wasn't enough information yet to reach a conclusion.

As Frank made the last turn for home, he noticed a set of headlights in his rearview mirror. He couldn't make out the other vehicle—the glare was too bright—but he noticed it kept a steady half-dozen car lengths behind him.

Pulling up in front of his house, Frank cut the engine and peered into his side mirror. The mystery vehicle had stopped about twenty yards back and sat idling, its lights still on. Frank climbed out of the van and watched as the other car—a long black limousine—pulled slowly beside him. When the darkened side rear window began to glide down, Frank tensed, ready for anything.

A voice sounded from the limo's dark interior. "Frank Hardy—step over here a moment, will you?"

There was something familiar about the voice, but Frank didn't like this at all—approaching an unidentified stranger hidden in the back of a limo at night.

"Who is it?" Frank asked, keeping his distance.

"Come on over where I can talk to you," the voice said.

"Not unless you say who you are," Frank said.

Frank started to walk away when a huge man jumped out of the front of the limo and grabbed him by the arm.

"My boss wants to talk to you," the chauffeur said. Before Frank could answer, the back door of the limo sprung open, and the chauffeur shoved him inside. He landed on the plush-carpeted floor next to a pair of well-shod feet. The door was slammed shut.

Chapter 6

"WELL, YOUNG MAN, it looks like we're going to have an opportunity to talk after all."

Frank looked up at the familiar face of Hans Hedrick. In the dim light from a street lamp, the fencing master smiled. "I have some important business to discuss with you, and time is of the essence."

"What's with all this cloak-and-dagger stuff?" Frank asked, hoisting himself onto the seat.

"Let's just say it's very important that I maintain the confidentiality of the information I am about to reveal to you," Hedrick said. "If you agree, we go for a ride and I can make you the offer, but you must give me your word that our conversation goes no further than here."

"So where are we going?" Frank said.

"Just for a drive. We need some time to chat."

From what little Frank had seen of Hedrick, he didn't like the man—and he certainly didn't trust him, either. He seemed arrogant and conceited, but was he also dangerous? Frank decided to take a chance because he was convinced that, at the very least, the old champion knew something about Ross's disappearance.

"Does this have anything to do with Adam Ross?" Frank asked.

The older man studied Frank through half-closed eyes, stroking his chin. "Unfortunately, I can't go into that just yet."

"But you will when the time comes?" Frank asked. Hedrick just looked at him with the hint of a smile that didn't say yes but didn't say no, either.

"All right," Frank said. "I'll listen to your offer. Let's go."

The burly driver, who had climbed back into the driver's seat, stomped on the accelerator. With a thrum of its powerful engine and a screech of rubber, the limo shot into the night.

As they sped through the streets of Bayport toward the expressway, Hedrick surprised Frank by paying him a major compliment. "You know, you're an extraordinarily talented fencer," he said.

"Thanks," Frank said, "but—"

"I'm serious," Hedrick went on. "Your timing, balance, quickness, and power are exceptional. I've seen enough prospects to know. You have lightning-fast reflexes. Believe me, with practice, you could become a top swordsman."

"Is this what you practically kidnapped me to say?" Frank asked.

"You'll understand its importance in a few moments." The older man paused. "What if I offered you a chance to join the best and most promising fencers in the world?"

Frank stared at his host. "Join them where? Doing what?"

"Several in your position have already said yes," Hedrick said. "My recruits, I call them. Believe me, they enjoy more time to train than anyone anywhere, and they live like princes. A world-class fencing facility is at their disposal, and, for fun, sports cars, motorcycles, private movie screening rooms, billiard tables, a bowling alley, indoor pool—not to mention more money than they can possibly spend."

"So that's where Ross is?" Frank asked.

Hedrick shrugged Frank's statement off, but then surprised him again when he said, "I'll admit this much—when I was missing briefly yesterday, I was making arrangements with Adam along these lines."

"Were you the one who put chloroform on

my mask? To get my brother and me off your trail?"

Hedrick smiled. "What makes you think that?"

"Just a wild guess. Plus that cologne you're wearing is the same stuff somebody used to try to disguise the chloroform. It's the last thing I smelled before I passed out on the strip. I noticed your driver was wearing it, too. I could smell it when he helped me into the car."

Hedrick smiled. "No harm in admitting it. We did doctor your mask. And your powers of observation—olfactory and otherwise—are impressive."

"It doesn't seem to bother you that I could have been hurt," Frank said.

"But you weren't, were you?" the older man said, and glanced out the window. Frank realized they were eight or nine miles outside of town, heading through marshlands that led to the bay, the airport—and nothing much else.

"Well," Hedrick said, "what's your answer? I invite you to join the most elite group of fencers in the world. You'll have everything you want, and all you need to do is train and fence. But you've got to let me know now. If you say no, you won't get another chance. This truly is a once-in-a-lifetime offer."

"You want me to sign up for some kind of

fencing school or team you're running?" Frank asked.

"Correct."

"And what do you want from me?" Frank said.

"Just your best effort to develop your potential as a top swordsman," Hedrick said.

"I'm going to need some more details," Frank said. "Like where are we going, how long do I sign up for—"

"I'm sorry, but I can't reveal any more until I have some kind of commitment from you," Hedrick said.

"So what if I agree to try out for this Hedrick Elite Swordsmanship School or whatever you're calling it," Frank said. "Then when I get there, I decide I don't like it, that I want to drop out?"

"We consider that an extremely remote possibility," Hedrick said. "Once you have a taste of what we have to offer, you won't want to turn back."

"And what if I say no?" Frank asked. The thought had occurred to him that they could easily dump him in the marsh if he didn't go along.

"Jerry, stop the car," Hedrick said. The limo swerved off onto the shoulder and came to a quick stop. "If you say no, you are free to go now, no questions asked, none answered. And your tremendous potential goes to waste." Hedrick reached out and put his hand on the door handle.

"So if I say no, you're going to drop me here, and I can hitch a ride home?"

"Frank, we're on a tight schedule," Hedrick said. "If you insist, I can drop you off at the main terminal of the airport, but that's as far as you go if you don't sign on."

Frank stopped to think. Things were starting to get interesting. If he said no, this case would practically end before it had even begun. It was hard to gauge the potential danger. Hedrick hadn't made any threats, but he certainly was being evasive. If only Frank could get a quick message to Joe, then he wouldn't have to worry about backup if something went wrong. I came this far, Frank thought, I might as well play along.

"Okay," Frank said. "I'll go along, but I reserve my right to quit anytime I want."

Hedrick immediately leaned forward and tapped the driver's shoulder twice. He hit the accelerator again and gunned the limo back onto the expressway. They got off at the next exit, following a sign that read Bayport Airport, 1 mile.

"So where *are* we going?" Frank said. "Now that I'm willing to join your team, why don't you tell me a little more about it?"

Hedrick just smiled again. "Don't be so inquisitive. You'll learn everything in time. And don't worry about needing anything—we'll provide everything you need."

"If we're going on a flight, I'd like to phone my family," Frank said.

"Sorry, we don't have time," Hedrick said. "We'll get to that later. For now, I offer my personal guarantee of your safety."

A few minutes later, the limo reached the main terminal. But it shot right past, continuing toward the private aviation section of the airport. The driver pulled the car up to the main building there, and Hedrick motioned for Frank to climb out.

"We've got to move quickly now," Hedrick said, checking his watch. "He'll be waiting for us."

"He who?" Frank asked. But Hedrick just rushed ahead, beckoning Frank to follow.

The private aviation terminal looked makeshift. It was built of cinder block and lit by long fluorescent-tube fixtures. Frank followed Hedrick down a short hallway that was still under construction and into a large room with a counter along one wall. A tall young woman in a red uniform was standing in front of a computer monitor.

"I don't recognize you," the coach said to her. "Are you new?"

So I guess you're kidnapping me after all," nk said.

Please, Frank, just relax," Hedrick said. "In e, you'll understand."

Me relax?" Frank said with a chuckle. ou're the one who's in such a big hurry. Are afraid we're going to miss your flight or ıething?"

gnoring Frank's remark, the older man led back past the counter and out an exit 'ked Hangar 2. Their footsteps echoed on pavement, and they continued out to where eek two-engine corporate jet was waiting.

Now can you at least tell me where we're ded?" Frank shouted above the plane's aming turbines.

Soon enough," Hedrick shouted back. With , he led Frank up the stairway and into the ıe and pulled the door shut behind them.

ɔe sat frowning at the telephone. His home-k lay spread across the kitchen table, but e Frank's strange call, he couldn't concen-. Their mom was upstairs watching a video :he VCR in her bedroom, and Aunt Ger-e was still out of town.

'ank had said he was with Hans Hedrick, that made no sense. He had gone out to get :za with Callie. And anyway, wasn't Hedrick in New York City or wherever he lived?

"Barbara called in sick," the young woman explained. "I'm Laurie. I'm filling in."

"Well, I'm Hans Hedrick, and we're ready to go. Is everything in order?"

The young woman smiled and tapped some keys on her computer console. But then her smile slipped.

"Um . . . I'm afraid I don't see your flight plan."

"What?" Hedrick snapped. "Come on, we're in a rush."

"I'm sorry," she said. "But the computers went down this afternoon, and they're still not entirely back up to speed. I'll have to feed the arrangements in manually. It shouldn't take too long."

"We don't have time for this," Hedrick said. "Where's your supervisor?"

"Back in the control room, sir."

"I'd like to see him right away." Hedrick turned to Frank. "Wait here. This'll take only a minute." And with that, he went off with the anxious young woman.

Frank had no intention of waiting. If Hedrick didn't give him the time to phone home, he'd just take it. As soon as Hedrick and the young woman disappeared through a door marked Private, Frank made an about-face and retraced his steps. He recalled passing a pay phone down the hall on the way in. He walked quickly around the corner, and there it was, near the entrance.

Frank glanced over his shoulder, lifted the receiver, slipped a quarter into the slot, and dialed home.

Hurry up, Frank thought, pressing the receiver to his ear and listening to the ring. He glanced over his shoulder, saw that the coast was still clear, and turned back to the phone, bending his head toward the floor.

Br-r-r-ing . . .

"Hello?"

"Joe," Frank said. "I only have a second. I'm with Hans Hedrick at the—"

Frank heard a sharp click followed by the drone of the dial tone. Somebody had reached over his shoulder and was holding down the hook with two fingers.

Chapter 7

FRANK TURNED AROUND and facec Hedrick.

"One of our main rules is no cont the outside world," Hedrick said, grat receiver and hanging it up.

"That's ridiculous," Frank said. "I calling my family. I figured they migh ally notice I was gone."

Hedrick took Frank's elbow and g away from the phone. "Frank, the ti in a young man's life to leave his fam to look to the future. Opportunitie come along once in a lifetime. To t tage of it, you must give it your fulles which means no outside distractions

Joe reached for the phone and dialed Callie's number. After two rings, he heard her familiar hello.

"Hi, Callie," Joe said.

"What's up, Joe?" Callie said.

"Callie, this may sound weird, but is Frank still there?"

She paused. "Is he here? No, he dropped me off more than an hour ago. You mean he's not back yet?"

"Oh, well," Joe began, "he probably stopped on the way home for a burger or something."

"Joe," Callie said, "we polished off a large pie at Mr. Pizza. I only ate two slices. Why don't you just tell me what's going on?"

"All right," Joe said, and he described Frank's call.

"I don't like the sound of this," Callie said. "What do you know about this Hedrick guy?"

"Not much," Joe said. "He's an ex-champion fencer, a show-off. He does some coaching now, and I don't trust him. I should get off the phone in case Frank tries to call back."

"Okay," Callie said. "But as soon as you hear from him, give me a call or have him call me."

"Will do, Callie. 'Bye." Joe hung up, then stood and started to pace.

What was Frank doing with Hans Hedrick? He wouldn't have set up a meeting without saying something first. Maybe it was a chance encounter. So why the frantic phone call, and who cut Frank off? And what about Adam Ross?

Joe paced into the front hall and looked out the window. Their van was parked right out front. Joe grabbed the spare keys from the kitchen hook and rushed out to the van. He opened the driver's side door and pulled the flashlight out of the glove compartment. Nothing seemed to be out of place.

Joe examined the inside of the van, got out and peered up underneath. Then he started combing the street. He took his time, but he couldn't find anything. If Frank had been abducted by force, there wasn't any sign of it.

Joe went back inside, totally puzzled. He needed to track down Hedrick. He called New York information, but that was a dead end. Next he tried Coach Kupcek, first at the *salle,* where a machine answered, and then at home.

"Coach," Joe said when he heard Kupcek's voice, "I'm sorry to call so late, but by any chance do you have Hans Hedrick's phone number?" Joe described Frank's strange call.

"So your brother's missing now, too?" Kupcek said. "Joe, I try to stay away from Hedrick. You saw how he acted at the tournament. I don't have his address or phone number. But I'll be in the *salle* tomorrow morning. If Frank's not back, come by, and we'll see what we can do."

"Okay, Coach—and thanks . . ."

Joe hung up. He didn't want to worry his mom, so he decided not to tell her Frank wasn't home yet. She'd assume he'd come in when she saw the van outside. Joe wasn't ready to call it a night yet, though. He went into his father's office, flicked on the computer, and went online to look Hedrick up in the crime records databases. By the time he'd run a full check and come up empty, it was past midnight, and he was exhausted. He looked at the phone on the desk beside him. Well, Frank had called to check in once—he'd definitely do it again as soon as he had the chance. Joe set his head on the desk to rest a moment.

Frank peered out the window and saw moonlit clouds streaming past like wisps of silver-blue cotton candy. It seemed unbelievable that just two hours earlier he had been enjoying a pizza with Callie. Now he was on a jet flying to . . . where, he had no idea. He could tell they had circled back inland after takeoff, then headed across the bay and out over the ocean on a course to the northeast.

Frank turned to Hans Hedrick, who was dozing beside him. He was surprised a few minutes later, when Hedrick, his eyes still closed, said, "Feeling restless?"

"I'm fine," he said. "Still waiting for you to let me know what's going on."

There was a click in front of them, and the cockpit door started to open.

Hedrick smiled. "Perfect timing."

The door swung open, and out stepped T. D. Brubaker, the billionaire fencing sponsor, who came toward him with an outstretched hand.

"Welcome," Brubaker said, shaking Frank's hand. "I'm glad you decided to join us."

"Mr. Hedrick says you can explain what this is all about," Frank said.

"Certainly." Brubaker leaned back and made a bridge with his fingers. "Hans works for me," he began. "He scouts tournaments to identify the best fencers on the circuit, then recruits them to join a very select group . . ." Brubaker took a long pause. "But I should start from the beginning. You probably know sport fencing developed out of the eighteenth-century tradition of fighting duels of honor. Well, I believe it's the most distinguished and aristocratic of sports, and I want to perpetuate its traditions.

"As a boy, I went to a boarding school that specialized in fencing. In fact, it's where I got this." Brubaker raised a finger to the fine, inch-long scar beneath his eye. "My own modest version of a Heidelberg scar."

"Heidelberg scar?" Frank asked.

"During World War One, the Heidelberg

Fencing Academy was the best in the world. Kings, presidents, and wealthy aristocrats sent their sons to learn the art of the sword. Many of the young men fenced with only half-masks, leaving one side of their faces uncovered."

"So they would get sliced," Frank said.

"Exactly," Brubaker said. "It was a badge of honor. They would even rub salt into the wound to make sure it scarred.

"I mention this only to show how fanatical I was. I even had hopes of going to the Olympics. But then my accident changed things. Torn ligaments in my shoulder when I was seventeen. I tried to come back too fast, reinjured my shoulder, and could never fence competitively again."

"That's tough," Frank said.

"Imagine if you tore up your shoulder and could never play baseball again," Brubaker said. "My family had money, but I didn't care. What I loved most had been taken away.

"I always thought fencers never got their due. Then I had an idea—since I couldn't fence, what if I gathered the best talent money could buy, a private 'stable,' and had them fence for me?

"I founded Castle Salle. Our team members lead a dream life: sports cars, motorcycles, plus the world's greatest fencing facility. All we ask is that you attend a formal dinner every night and do what you love—fence. It's the perfect way to give the most talented young swordsmen the recognition they deserve." Brubaker smiled broadly. "Sound too good to be true? Well, it isn't. It exists, and I created it. So to answer your question, we're headed to the fencing capital of the world: Heidelberg, Germany."

"Heidelberg?" Frank said.

"That's right," Brubaker replied. "Now, I'll let you rest. It's late, and you have a long day ahead of you. Welcome to the team."

With that, Brubaker reached up and flicked off the light. Frank sat in the darkened cabin, the silver-blue moonlight filling the window, for a long time before he dozed off.

The Sunday morning light streamed in through Fenton Hardy's office window, and Joe lifted his head off his arms. He blinked at the wall clock. Seven o'clock. He stood up and rubbed his neck as he headed for Frank's room, where the bed was still made. He hadn't come home. Joe headed for the front door.

"Joe?" Laura Hardy said, coming from her bedroom. "Where's Frank?"

"He, uh, called late last night—it must have been after you went to sleep. He stayed at Chet's. See you, Mom."

Outside, Joe climbed into the van and headed for the Bayport Salle to see if Coach Kupcek could help him track down Frank.

"I take it there's been no word from Frank?" Kupcek said as he let Joe into the studio.

"Not a word, Coach," Joe said.

"Something occurred to me this morning—I'm sure Hedrick's a member of the USFA, that's the United States Fencing Association." At his cluttered desk, he began sifting through business cards. "Ah, here we are." He handed Joe a card. "They're based in Washington, D.C. There won't be anyone in their office now, but the director's name is Pete Shelley."

Joe got Shelley's home number from information. He called and left a message on Shelley's answering machine.

"What do you know about those three other fencers who disappeared?" Joe said as he hung up.

"Just their names—Brett Stanton, Bob Gale, and Carlos DeMarco," Kupcek said. "Do you think there's some connection with Frank and Adam?"

"It's possible. Let's see what we can find out."

Coach Kupcek called around to his friends at other fencing clubs, taking notes at his desk.

"Okay," Kupcek said when he finally hung up. "Unfortunately, Brett Stanton was killed in a rock-climbing accident six months ago. I got a number for Carlos DeMarco and an address for Bob Gale."

"Let's try DeMarco," Joe said, taking the slip of paper from Kupcek and dialing the number.

"Yes?" said a woman who answered on the first ring.

"I'm trying to reach Carlos DeMarco," Joe said. "My brother's a fencer, and—"

"So you haven't heard about Carlos?" the woman said. "He's been missing for four months. I'm his aunt Gina. His parents are dead. He used to live in my house—sometimes but not always. I filed a missing persons report with the police, but they never did anything about it. At least, they never called me back. I can't imagine why. Poor Carlos. Maybe he'll turn up, maybe he won't. What am I supposed to do? I'm seventy-three years old. I'm a widow. Carlos is a very independent young man, but at least he should call—"

"Thank you, ma'am. I'm terribly sorry to bother you," Joe said, and hung up. "Phew. Okay, what about Bob Gale?"

"His club only had an address," Kupcek said, handing Joe a slip of paper. Joe tried information, but the number was unlisted.

"This isn't too far from here," Joe said, looking at the address. "Want to take a drive?"

"Why not?" Kupcek said.

They headed north out of Bayport on winding country roads. Within half an hour, they found their turnoff, a small dirt road. The van bounced over muddy ruts, and overgrown branches swiped at the windshield. Finally, they found a rugged cabin in a partial clearing back in the woods. There were oak and maple trees growing right up to its doorstep, as if guarding the entrance.

Joe and Coach Kupcek climbed down from the van and approached the heavy wooden door of the cabin.

Joe knocked sharply. No answer. He tried again, yelling out, "Anybody home?"

"Looks like no one's around," Kupcek finally said.

"One more try," Joe said, banging hard with his palm this time. "Hey, anybody—"

There was a zinging sound that grew instantly loud. Joe saw a flash of metal and heard a thunk as an arrow hit the door and quivered inches from his head. Then he heard another zing and shouted, "Get down!"

Chapter 8

JOE AND THE COACH both hit the dirt as the second arrow buried itself in a tree next to the cabin with a thwack.

A moment later there was rustling at the edge of the woods, and a tall young man in full camouflage gear appeared. He held a stubby compound hunting bow in his hand.

"Hey!" Joe shouted. "Hold your fire!"

The young man came toward Joe, grinning. "Scared you, huh?"

"You almost killed me," Joe said.

"I wasn't trying to hit you—just come close," the young man said. "You were scared, though, admit it."

Joe felt like grabbing the stranger and pounding some sense into him. Coach Kupcek got up and said, "All right, maybe you can help us. We're looking for Bob Gale."

"That's me," the stranger said.

"We understand you used to fence a lot, but then you dropped off the circuit," Joe said. "We were wondering why."

"Fencing got boring." Gale shrugged. "Too many rules, too much practice. Hey, I'm into much cooler stuff now." He held up the bow. "I've got bolas, spears, crossbows. Want to check them out?"

"We'll pass," Joe said.

"You sure?"

"Positive," Joe said. "We were also wondering about some of the other fencers who dropped out—Brett Stanton, Carlos DeMarco . . . have you heard anything about them?"

"Are you guys cops or something?" Gale said.

"No," Kupcek said. "I'm Laslo Kupcek, owner of the Bayport Salle. This is Joe Hardy. We're looking for Joe's brother, Frank."

Gale twanged the empty bow string. "I've heard of DeMarco, but that's it. He was supposed to be real good. He left the circuit just before I did, but I don't know where he went. Hey, I'm going to do some target practice. Want to join me?"

"No thanks," Joe said, turning toward the van. "We've got to go."

Joe and Kupcek got into the van without another word and drove away. "Come again anytime," Gale yelled. "I don't get a lot of visitors out here."

Looking at Gale in the rearview mirror, Joe muttered, "Gee, that's a surprise."

Back at the *salle,* they had a message from the USFA director, Pete Shelley. Joe returned the call right away, explaining that he needed to contact Hans Hedrick.

"Well, I have a mailing address for him," the director said after a brief search of his database, "but it isn't exactly local. In fact, it's in Heidelberg."

"Heidelberg, *Germany?"* Joe said.

"That's right," the director answered, and he spelled out the address and phone number for Joe.

"Thanks," Joe said. "And by the way, do you know anything about a fencer named Carlos DeMarco?"

"Only that he disappeared four months ago. I hear the FBI and Interpol are looking for him, but they haven't turned up anything yet."

Joe thanked the director again, said goodbye, and hung up.

"What now?" Coach Kupcek asked.

"I'm taking a little trip to Germany," Joe

said, picking up the phone and dialing information.

"What?" Kupcek said.

"The number for the Quick Flite Travel Agency, please," Joe said into the receiver.

"Don't you think we should check with the German police," Kupcek said, "try to track Hedrick down? You're going to waste a ticket and—"

"They might tip him off," Joe said. "The only way to handle this is to confront him face-to-face. I've got my passport in the van, and I've got plenty of frequent flyer miles, so it's no cash out of my pocket."

Kupcek nodded. "All right. Book me a ticket, too. If you've got the miles."

"Coach, I appreciate the gesture, but—"

"Joe," Kupcek said. "Do you speak German?"

Joe admitted he didn't.

"Well, I do," the coach said. "And, in fact, I'd like to make a call to Heidelberg right now."

Joe handed him the piece of paper with Hedrick's phone number on it. The coach dialed and had a brief conversation in German.

"We're in luck," Kupcek said after he hung up. "He's in Germany."

"How do you know? What did you say?" Joe said.

"I called and got the housekeeper," Kupcek said. "I said I was the dry cleaner with a rush order for Mr. Hedrick's suit alterations and asked her if he'd be home tomorrow for delivery. She said yes, he was due in this morning from overseas."

"Pretty slick, Coach," Joe said. "Are you sure you don't have any investigative experience?"

Kupcek chuckled and said, "No, I guess I just sound like a dry cleaner. Let's book our flights."

Frank felt a bump and opened his eyes. Morning light filtered in through the window next to his seat, and he looked out to see the runway rushing past just beneath the jet's wing.

"Welcome to Heidelberg," Brubaker said. Frank turned to see the wealthy businessman smiling. Hans Hedrick, also awake, was adjusting his tie.

As they deplaned, a limo identical to the one that had dropped them off at the Bayport Airport the night before glided to a stop. A young chauffeur sprang out, touched his cap, and opened the door for them.

As the limo sped through the countryside, Frank admired the scenery and wondered how they'd gotten through Customs. Then he decided that when you were as rich as Brubaker, you didn't have to bother with Customs. Rolling fields dotted with picturesque little farms gave way to a forest of big pine trees. Before long, Frank picked out a castle on a hill in the distance. Built of huge stones, complete with crenellation and imposing turrets, it looked like a remnant of medieval times.

"Castle Salle, just up ahead," Brubaker announced proudly as they came closer. "Meticulously restored to look exactly as it did six centuries ago."

The limo turned off at a gatehouse and climbed a winding road through the pine forest. They pulled into the castle courtyard over a bridge across a moat. Frank saw a half-dozen gleaming sports cars parked inside. They were of various makes and models, and their bright colors contrasted strikingly with the gray stone of the ancient castle.

The butler bowed as he admitted them into the entryway, which boasted a soaring forty-foot ceiling, barred windows, and torches on the walls.

"We spared no expense to install modern training facilities," Brubaker said, his voice echoing in the vast space. "Hans, why don't you go rest up for a while. I'll show Frank the gym."

Hedrick went off with a wave of his hand, and Frank followed Brubaker's energetic footsteps. They walked through several wide hallways to a *salle* much like Coach Kupcek's, only newer and larger. In addition to fencing facilities, it had tumbling mats, free weights, and gymnastics equipment. Five young men, two on a fencing strip holding swords, turned toward them as they entered.

"Excellent," Brubaker said. "You can meet some of the others. . . ."

All five were about Frank's age and wearing unbuttoned fencing jackets. They stiffened when they saw Brubaker.

"Gentlemen," Brubaker said. "Meet our newest recruit—Frank Hardy. Frank, meet Jean Broussard, Zach Barns, and Carlos DeMarco. . . ."

Frank recognized DeMarco's name right away as one of the circuit dropouts mentioned in New York. He wondered if all the other dropouts were Brubaker "recruits," too. Frank nodded at DeMarco, and the dark-haired, brown-eyed fencer smiled back.

"And this is Vince Beatty," Brubaker continued, "and senior fencer Friedrich Schiller." Schiller, the tallest of the group, gave Frank a powerful handshake.

"Warming up for three o'clock practice?" Brubaker asked. "Carry on, gentlemen. Don't let me interrupt."

Beatty and Broussard faced each other again on the strip. Schiller stepped forward, and ordered the salute, and the fencers resumed.

Frank was surprised that Beatty had a saber while Broussard wielded a much lighter, old-fashioned rapier in his right hand and a dagger in his left. Though Beatty had just the one blade, he slashed hard, keeping Broussard at bay. As they went at it, Beatty lunged, but the smaller, quicker Broussard used the dagger to parry, then counterattacked with the rapier.

All in all, the two seemed well matched—and they were among the best Frank had ever seen. They both had superb footwork, balance, and hand speed.

After a few minutes of give-and-take, Broussard mounted a strong attack, and his heavy-bladed saber slash proved too much for Beatty. The dagger flew from Beatty's grip, and Broussard swung his weapon at his foe's midsection, stopping the blade an inch short of the other's white jacket.

"Bravo," Brubaker said. "Well done."

"They use different weapons?" Frank asked.

"It's a form of cross-training," the castle owner replied. "Instead of practicing with just the three standard blades, my fencers use all kinds—cutlasses, rapiers, broadswords, even maces and battle-axes." Brubaker led Frank back out to the main hall, where the butler waited.

Frank decided to follow up on the introductions by asking about his Bayport teammate. "And Adam Ross—is he here, too?"

Brubaker's eyes narrowed. "Brian," he said, turning to the butler, "show Frank his room.

"Settle in, but come to the three o'clock practice," the billionaire said to Frank. "No need to join in, just watch closely." Brubaker turned and left.

Frank followed the butler out of the gym and up a stone spiral staircase, then to a hallway with heavy wooden doors.

"This is the dormitory floor," Brian said. Stopping at one door, he lifted the latch. "And here is your room."

The room was twice as big as Frank's bedroom at home, with a large canopy bed and heavy oak bureau, mirror, and desk set. There was also a wide-screen TV, a VCR, a stereo system, and an elaborate clock-radio, but no phone. Outside the second-story window, the thickly forested hill fell off sharply, yielding a commanding view of the countryside.

"The tailor will measure you for shirts, slacks, jackets, and custom-made fencing suits tomorrow," Brian said. "And we have a shoesmith on the premises. Don't forget—practice is at three. Mr. Brubaker appreciates punctuality." With that, he left.

Frank looked around the room, examining the electronic equipment, which was all state-of-the-art. If Brubaker meant to keep his fencers happy with expensive toys, this was a good start.

Well, Frank thought, his latest attempt to find out more about Adam Ross had led nowhere.

But right now, he had another priority—to let Joe know where he was.

Checking the time, he saw he had only twenty-five minutes until practice. All he needed was a few moments on a phone.

Opening the door, Frank gazed up and down the hallway. It was empty.

He slipped out, closed the door, and made his way down the corridor. Most of the other doors were also closed. From behind the one that was slightly ajar came the beat of heavy metal music. Frank slipped quietly past.

Halfway down the hallway, he came to a niche with a window and a small table beneath it. He was amazed to see a telephone in plain sight on the table. He was about to pick up the receiver when a door slammed down the hall. Frank looked up and saw Carlos DeMarco leaving his room.

"Hey, Carlos," Frank said, turning as if he'd been looking out the window. "Isn't this view something? Are you going to practice?"

Carlos smiled as he approached. "Yep. I'm heading to the locker room to change."

"I'll walk down there with you, if that's okay," Frank said.

"Fine. Let's take the back stairs—it's quicker."

The locker room was one of the best equipped Frank had ever seen.

"You seem to know the castle layout pretty well," Frank said. "Have you been here awhile?"

DeMarco's smile wavered. "We're not supposed to talk about that."

"About what?"

"Ourselves. Our pasts. It's one of Mr. Brubaker's rules. We just concentrate on our fencing and fighting skills."

"I just wondered how long you've been in the program," Frank said. "That's about fencing, isn't it?"

DeMarco stood looking at Frank uncomfortably.

The door opened, and several others came in—Broussard, Barns, and the big senior fencer, Schiller.

"Ready for tonight's bout?" Barns asked Broussard.

"As ready as I'll ever be," Broussard said. "That was a good workout today."

"The audience is supposed to be huge," said Barns, who wore tortoise-shell glasses. Frank thought he was the most relaxed and easygoing of Brubaker's team.

"Will you all—I mean, will *we* all be competing?" Frank asked.

"Oh, no," Broussard answered in his slight French accent. "Public tournaments are for Monsieur Brubaker's second-string fencers.

We're the first string. We fence only private bouts."

"Private bouts like tonight's?" Frank asked.

"You ask too many questions," came a gruff voice.

Frank turned and saw Schiller scowling at him. He stood at his locker bare-chested, his heavy shoulders and thick biceps marked by scars.

"Excuse me?" Frank said.

"I said stop asking questions. You should be glad you were selected," Schiller said.

"I'm just trying to find out what I'm supposed to be doing here," Frank said. "Do you have a problem with that?"

Suddenly, Schiller slammed his locker door, the sound echoing as explosively as a gunshot in the hard-surfaced room.

"You didn't hear me, did you?" Schiller shouted. "I said mind your business."

"Fine," Frank said. "As long as you mind yours."

Schiller flung his jacket aside and charged Frank with his fists clenched.

Chapter 9

FRANK WANTED to take Schiller down with a quick judo move as he'd done with Adam Ross in their saber sparring session at the Bayport Salle. Then he remembered he might be here awhile, so he decided to keep the peace.

"Whoa, hold it," Frank said. He stood his ground and held up his palms. "I'm new here. Of course I've got questions. Calm down, Schiller, and maybe we can settle this without anybody getting hurt."

Schiller was right in Frank's face now. "All right, but you'd better watch yourself," he growled. Then, turning to the others, he said, "Anyone else have any questions?"

Schiller glared from face to face until it was obvious no one would speak up.

"Well, that's it, then," Schiller said. "We might as well get on with practice—let's go, everybody."

Frank spent the rest of the afternoon watching the others in the big gym. Practice began with Hedrick leading his fencers through drills. Hedrick shouted his commands like an army sergeant, correcting the young men's mistakes in harsh tones: "No jumping or rocking," he roared. "Keep those backs straight, all movements smooth." At one point, he snatched Jean Broussard's sword to jab the young man's foot.

"*Always* keep that front foot pointed forward!" Hedrick shouted. "In preparation, on guard, and advance. You know that, Broussard. Remember, if it's on a diagonal, you've got no stability, no accuracy, and you look clumsy. Now straighten it."

Next came advanced techniques, many of them new to Frank. Using the glide attack, the fencers slid their weapons quickly along an opponent's blade to get in close.

"Don't forget," Hedrick said, "your enemy's sword must be horizontal and his sword arm fully extended." They practiced the *balestra,* a jump-and-lunge move that allowed a fencer to cover a great distance quickly, and the *fleche,* a low-line attack in which the fencer stabbed from a deep lunge.

Several times the door would open and Brubaker would come in. Picking up a sword, he would stand on the sidelines, rest it on his shoulder, and watch. During one visit, as DeMarco and Barns fenced, Brubaker told Schiller to take DeMarco's place. Before they began, Brubaker whispered into Schiller's ear.

"All right," Brubaker said a moment later, "Fence."

Frank could tell immediately that Barns was good, but Schiller was better. Schiller attacked viciously, and though Barns defended well, the senior fencer kept up his relentless attack, finally forcing the young fencer off the strip. Schiller kept advancing, even though the younger man lowered his sword, expecting the attack to cease when his foot left the strip. But Schiller struck Barns's sword hard, knocking the blade to the floor. Then he pressed the point of his weapon to Barns's chest, and the younger man stared, open-mouthed, his back arched against a pommel horse as Schiller seemed about to plunge his sword into his throat.

"Okay, that's it," Brubaker said. Stepping forward, he pushed Schiller's blade aside, clapped him on the back, and chuckled. "Excellent, Friedrich. But we don't want to be one fencer short tonight."

Turning to his fencers, the castle owner said, "And there's another lesson for you—never show your opponent mercy, and don't expect any from him. You're here to become fighting machines. I picked you because you're the best, but to stay the best takes work. You've got to develop a warrior's spirit: focused, relentless, without mercy.

"Think about what we do here. Isn't everyone's wish, deep down, to score a total victory, with no restrictions or limitations? To show what you're made of? Right here, besides the best instruction anywhere, the lavish lifestyle, the money, and the chance to become world champions in hand-to-hand combat, you get something more—a chance to defy death itself."

Frank had to admit Brubaker was a captivating speaker. He spoke with dramatic pauses and flourishes, his intense stare seeming to draw each student in. Whether or not Frank agreed with it, he sensed the appeal of Brubaker's program.

"Well, gentlemen," Brubaker said, "keep up the good work. And I'll see you all at dinner." He turned and walked out.

The students fenced for the rest of the afternoon, taking only short breaks, during which they chatted about fencing, arguing over brands of equipment, styles of sword grips, which country produced the best blades, and so on. Frank realized these were true fanatics, their thoughts and conversations rarely straying from the subject of sword fighting.

Eventually, Coach Hedrick clapped his hands three times and announced, "All right, enough for today. I don't want you to wear yourselves out for tonight. Let's shower up."

At the fencer's caddy, a multiwheeled cart that stored their equipment, Frank looked up and saw Carlos DeMarco and Vince Beatty.

"By the way, we dress for dinner," DeMarco said.

"Mr. Brubaker mentioned that," Frank said. "I got fitted for a suit this morning."

"That wasn't for just a suit—it was for a *tuxedo,*" Beatty said. "It's Brubaker's rule, formal wear at dinner." Beatty shrugged and smiled. "Since he buys the clothes, why not? You'll get used to the tux. Just don't be late: seven o'clock sharp in the main dining room."

Frank returned to his room to find a new tuxedo hanging in his closet. On the bureau sat a shirt and tie. It seemed amazing that Brubaker had gone to all this expense, but then who knew how much money the man had? Castle Salle might be just a small item in his overall budget.

The glowing blue letters on Frank's digital clock read six-forty as he began to dress for dinner.

* * *

The dining room was large and very elegant. Beneath a chandelier suspended from the tall ceiling sat two long, linen-covered tables, each with approximately a dozen settings of crystal and shining silver. About half the places were occupied already as the rest of the tuxedo-clad young fencers were filing in. Frank counted twenty places in all; there were all the familiar faces along with several he hadn't seen yet. The room had high windows with thick curtains, and off to the side Frank was surprised to see a live string quartet consisting of two violins, a viola, and a cello.

When Brubaker spotted Frank at the door, the host beckoned him over. "Good to see you, Frank," he said. "You're right on time. Have a seat over here." Frank took his place beside Brubaker. He noticed Hedrick holding court at the other table.

"I think you'll enjoy this," Brubaker said. "I spare no expense in keeping my fencers well nourished."

The food was excellent. First there was a crabmeat appetizer, then garden salad, followed by roast duck with vegetables and potatoes, all deliciously prepared. There was more low-key chat about fencing techniques and equipment, punctuated by leisurely pauses when everyone just sat back and enjoyed the sumptuous feast.

"Save some room for the Black Forest cake,

gentlemen; it's superb," Brubaker said halfway through the main course. Then he leaned back in his chair and cleared his throat. "You know, I couldn't be happier with Coach Hedrick's fencing instruction, but there's another side of the sport I don't want you gentlemen to neglect—its history, which influences customs and dress even today.

"How many of you know, for instance, why in high-class society a lady customarily takes a gentlemen's *left* arm?"

Frank spoke up. "The men needed to keep their right arms free to draw their swords." He remembered that from one of Coach Kupcek's lessons.

"Good, Frank," Brubaker said. "I see you have a well-rounded education." He paused, then addressed the rest of the group. "Fencing's still influential in other ways, too. Men's coats are buttoned left over right, for instance, so they're quick to open with the left hand and the right can reach for a sword. And the buttons on the backs of dress coats were originally designed to support a sword belt. You all know that men used to wear capes, but did you know it was to tangle up an enemy's sword, or throw into his face so he couldn't see as you ran him through?" Brubaker smiled at the group. "Any questions?"

"I have a few," Frank said.

"Well, let's have them," Brubaker said with a curious smile.

"First of all," Frank said, "how long have you been running this *salle?* Second, what happens when someone wants to leave? Also, who's going to be at tonight's match? And where's Adam Ross?"

Brubaker's smile tightened. "I believe we were talking about the history of our sport." He sat back and brought his napkin to his mouth. "A good meal puts one in a philosophical frame of mind. You know the thing I hate most? Waste. Waste not, want not, that's my motto. Never destroy or discard a valuable resource. Environmentalists talk of clean air and water and rain forests, but there are other kinds of natural resources. Talent, for instance. Think of yourselves. Few people can fence like you young men. Talent is *your* natural resource. And not to spend as much time developing it as possible—well, that would be a waste.

"If I own a resource, I never waste it. If I can't use it right away, I save it until I can. That applies to the rain forests, and to pretty much everything else, too."

The musicians were beginning a new piece, and Brubaker held up a finger. "Ah, Haydn's string quartet in D, one of my favorites."

The Black Forest cake was served, and, as promised, it was delicious. They all dug in and cleaned their plates, washing the cake down with cups of Jamaican Blue Mountain coffee, the perfect complement.

After dinner, as they filed out, Brubaker said to Frank, "About tonight's match . . . you're not required to be there the whole time—come at, say, ten-fifteen. The auditorium and arena are behind the main gym. Use the back entrance, the red door. Take a left just inside the main entrance, and you can't miss it."

Later that evening Frank made his way backstage as Brubaker had instructed. He heard cheers and applause punctuated by the loud ring of metal on metal. When he knocked at the red door, Hans Hedrick let him in.

"Good," Hedrick said. "Mr. Brubaker said you'd be coming to watch. Stand here, and you'll be able to see the arena. The next two will be right out."

Frank was in the curtained wings of a theater that looked out on what seemed to be a boxing ring, except it was octagonal in shape and had a six-foot wire-link fence on all sides. He tried to look out at the audience, but the powerful footlights were so blinding that he could barely see past the front of the stage. To judge by the volume of cheers and gasps, though, it was sizable.

Frank saw the fencers enter from the opposite

wing. First came Jean Broussard, wearing an odd costume: a sleeveless leather vest with baggy pirate's pantaloons and boots. He was pitted against an opponent Frank had never seen before, a tall, burly young man who looked to be in his early twenties. Frank assumed he might be from another sponsor's stable.

As they faced off, Frank noticed two things even more surprising than the costumes. First, neither wore a mask or protective padding, and second, although Broussard held a pirate's cutlass, his opponent wielded a large, heavy-looking battle-ax and shield.

"What's going on?" Frank asked Hedrick, standing nearby. "I thought those were only for cross-training."

"We find that mixing weapons and styles of combat makes the bouts more interesting," Hedrick explained.

As if confirming this, a loud cheer arose from the audience as the two contestants saluted each other.

"And what are all those about?" Frank asked, pointing out some reddish brown stains on the floor of the ring. He knew bloodstains when he saw them.

Hedrick glanced quickly at Frank, "Occasionally, accidents happen."

The crowd roared again as the two combatants charged at each other to start the bout.

Broussard was quick with the cutlass, but his opponent was well practiced with his ax, too. He swung the heavy blade in round arcs, so that it was always moving or poised for attack. Broussard stayed out of range, but barely, and when he darted in, his opponent thwarted his lunges with the shield. In all, Frank thought, it looked incredibly like the real thing: brutal and barbaric, exciting and dangerous.

Frank watched the first five minutes of the bout. The action was fast and furious, the contestants' concentration intense. He was fascinated. Before long, a voice sounded in his ear. "That's enough for tonight, Frank." He turned to see Hedrick leaning close. "Mr. Brubaker just wanted you to get a glimpse of the action so you know what to expect," the coach said. "You should leave now. Go back to your room, or go to the gym and get in a workout."

Frank began to object, saying he would rather watch Broussard's bout, but Hedrick firmly grasped his elbow and turned him toward the door. "You'll have plenty of exposure to live action soon enough."

Frank headed for the door, but seeing that Hedrick had turned back to the bout, he couldn't help lingering. No doubt it was all staged, like professional wrestling. The blades had to be dulled, and the two fighters must have been pretending to go at each other so fiercely.

It looked convincing, though, and Frank found it hard to tear himself away.

After watching another couple of minutes of fierce combat, Frank decided not to risk any more trouble. He'd just follow Hedrick's orders and lie low until he had a better idea of what was going on.

As he turned toward the door again, he heard the audience gasp. He spun around in time to see the big guy's ax come crashing down on Broussard, who let out an agonizing grunt as he crashed to the floor of the caged ring.

Chapter 10

"WHAT WAS THAT?" Frank asked. His adrenaline pumping, he took five quick strides toward the ring. As he passed Hedrick, the coach shot out a hand and grabbed his arm. "Frank, I thought I told you to leave."

"Broussard could be in trouble," Frank said. "I've got some emergency training, and—"

"You do as you're told." Hedrick tightened his grip and pulled Frank toward the door. "Any injuries will be attended to. All you're going to do is get in the way. Now get out of here." He shoved Frank out the door and slammed it.

Frank stood in the hallway and felt his heart racing. He hadn't seen enough to tell whether

Broussard was hurt badly or not. All he'd seen out of the corner of his eye was the ax coming down and then Broussard crashing to the floor. He looked back at the red door, paused, then slowly turned and walked toward the gym.

What kind of operation was Brubaker running here? What was with these weird reenactments of pirate battles? Was the axing just another of those "accidents" that left bloodstains in the ring? Who was in the audience?

Frank had a lot of questions. When he got to the gym, he kept going over them in his mind; there was no way he felt like practicing. He picked up a saber and felt its weight in his hands. He could hear the audience cheering again. When Broussard had gone down, the audience hadn't seemed fazed at all. They had shouted and whistled—some had even booed, come to think of it—as if it was exactly what they were expecting. And now they were at it again.

Frank raised the saber and took some half-hearted swipes. He bent his knees and lunged once or twice, but his heart wasn't in it. He was listening to the cheers, boos, whistles, and catcalls drifting in through the gym's open double doors. After a while, there was silence. It stretched for half a minute, then a minute and more. Frank stood with his saber raised, not moving, just listening. It was still quiet. Well, they must be done for the night. He raised his eyes to the mesh-covered wall clock. Eleven o'clock.

Frank heard footsteps in the hallway. He kept his eye on the doorway and instinctively tightened his grip on the saber. Carlos DeMarco appeared, and though he wasn't wearing pirate clothes like Broussard and his opponent, he did have on an old-fashioned outfit consisting of a ruffled white shirt, black knickers, and shoes with large silver buckles. DeMarco was sweaty, as if he'd been fencing. He wore a towel draped over one shoulder; his face was pale, and he was blinking nervously.

"Carlos, what happened?" Frank asked. "How's Broussard?"

DeMarco managed a weak smile. "Coach Hedrick says it looked worse than it was, that the ax blade was blunt and it wasn't a direct hit. I guess he has a broken collarbone, but they say he'll be okay."

"Well, he's lucky," Frank said. "It could have been a lot worse. What's the deal out there, anyway? They were really going at it—without safety equipment. And that audience was going wild."

"Well, you know," Carlos said, "the money gets them excited." He took the towel from his shoulder and wiped his forehead. He was gradually catching his breath.

"What money?" Frank asked.

"From the betting."

"There's gambling?"

"You didn't know?" Carlos said.

"They bet on bouts with live blades and no protection?" Frank said. "That's practically a guarantee that somebody's going to get hurt."

"Hey, Frank, Mr. Brubaker and Coach Hedrick have discussed this a lot. In the end, it's no different from betting on football or basketball."

"Carlos, football players wear helmets and shoulder pads, and they don't swing battle-axes."

"But we're highly skilled, specially trained athletes," DeMarco said. "Much more so than the kids in those other sports."

It was hard for Frank to believe DeMarco was accepting this so casually. "Don't you see?" he said. "This is crazy. It's not just a sport here—it's like Roman gladiators fighting at the Colosseum two thousand years ago."

"Oh, come on," DeMarco said. "You're making it sound like it's the Christians and the lions all over again. But we can handle ourselves."

Frank could see he wasn't getting anywhere with that line of reasoning, so he decided to try another angle. "Carlos, do you know a fencer named Adam Ross? He may have arrived in the last day or two."

DeMarco stopped cold. Was that a flicker of recognition Frank read on his face? Before DeMarco could answer, though, they heard footsteps approaching. They turned and saw Friedrich Schiller, who was also dressed in duelist's garb and looked sweaty and flushed. Frank noticed a blood smear on his shirt.

Schiller acknowledged Frank with little more than a grunt, then he turned to DeMarco. "Coach Hedrick wants to see you now. Let's go."

As DeMarco turned toward the door, Frank nodded at Schiller's shirt. "Have an accident?"

Schiller glanced down. "Not me." He smiled wryly and turned to follow DeMarco out.

Alone again, Frank figured he had another chance to find a phone so he could get in touch with Joe and fill him in. There had to be one around somewhere.

Frank left the gym and headed for the stairs. He climbed to the second-floor dormitory level, paused, then continued up to the third floor. A sign on the landing read Private—No Admittance.

Frank saw a long, dimly lit hallway with no windows and fewer wall sconces than downstairs. It took his eyes a couple of seconds to adjust to the darkness, then he spotted someone standing against the wall. He started to back off but then realized that the figure was actually a suit of armor, gleaming dully, half hidden in a shallow alcove. There were two doors in the hallway—one opposite the knight, the other at the far end. Frank crept down the hall cautiously.

The first door was made of rough-finished wood and came to a point at the top. It was hung with huge black iron hinges. Pressing his ear to it, Frank thought he heard someone moving about inside, but the sound was so muffled, he couldn't be sure. He decided not to take a chance and continued down the hall.

Frank listened at the other door. This time, he didn't hear anything. He tried the knob, but it wouldn't turn. He rooted through his pockets and found a paper clip. Bending the tip, he slipped it into the cylinder and started twisting. He worked the lock for several moments before hearing a welcome click. Easing the door open, he peered inside.

He saw a plush office bathed in the glow of a single table lamp. It had oak paneling and bookshelves lining one wall. To his left was a huge desk, and to his right were floor-length crimson velvet window curtains. An incredible array of weapons covered the wall—swords, daggers, battle-axes, and maces, along with several pairs of manacles—making the room look like an ancient armory. A desktop computer looked as out of place in there as the sports cars had in front of the castle. Frank guessed this was Brubaker's personal office. Next to the computer was the other modern appliance that Frank was looking for—a telephone.

As Frank eased the door shut behind him, he heard a retractable spring bolt snap shut. He crossed to the desk and snatched up the receiver. No sooner had he punched several buttons than he heard a whooping tone. He wasn't going to get anywhere without the access code. And he didn't want to chance taking a guess, because he might tip someone off that he was snooping around.

Sometimes people wrote their codes in obvious places so they wouldn't have to remember them. Frank scanned the desktop, noting an expensive-looking pen and pencil set, an oversize antique paperweight key, a brass tableclock, and, beside the computer, an ornately carved wooden cigar box with a gold cigarette lighter engraved T.D.B. on top of it.

He put the receiver back on the hook and focused on the computer. He could try sending Joe an e-mail message. Flicking on the power switch, Frank heard the soft whir of the hard drive and the crackle of static as the screen warmed up. A few seconds later he heard a startup beep, and familiar icons filled the screen. Frank was happy to see that even if Brubaker had password-protected individual files, he hadn't bothered to do so with the overall operating system. He scanned the menu, which listed financial spreadsheets, investment planners, and other business applications along with a number of games, including Sword Master, En Garde, and Samurai Warrior. Most of them involved fencing and fighting. No surprise there. He tapped the keyboard to access the modem software. After a few seconds, the screen's flashing green prompt read, Your Password?

Frank sat back and started to consider his options when he heard a sound through the thick office door—it was the unmistakable jangle of keys.

After darting his hand out to flick off the computer, Frank skirted the desk, went over to the window, and ducked behind the heavy curtains just as the door opened. He grabbed the folds to keep them from swaying, leaving a tiny gap that he could peer through.

T. D. Brubaker stepped in, a man at his leisure. He moved behind his desk and, still standing, lifted the lid of the ornate wooden box to take out a cigar, which he sniffed. Seeming to be satisfied, he removed a small cigar cutter from his pocket, snipped off the stogie's tip, and reached down for his lighter—in the same motion snapping on the computer's power switch. The billionaire brought the cigar to his mouth and flicked the lighter, but he had hardly started to puff when the computer beeped. It was up and running almost instantly, Frank realized, because it was already warmed up. Would Brubaker notice? The businessman stopped and stared at the screen. Then, removing the cigar from his mouth, he slowly reached out his hand to touch the computer's vents, which would still be warm.

Frank held his breath.

Slowly, Brubaker straightened up. Frank couldn't see his eyes, but his posture was tense and alert.

Brubaker turned to the wall behind him and lifted a long, heavy broadsword with a gleaming five-inch-wide blade from its mounting. Then his eyes scanned the room, coming to rest on the curtain.

Brubaker moved quickly and carefully, straight toward Frank. His elbow high, the billionaire raised the sword to the ready position with its tip perfectly positioned to skewer an opponent. Reaching out with his free hand, Brubaker yanked the curtains aside, and Frank found himself staring at the deadly point of the gleaming blade, inches from his right eyeball.

Chapter 11

"WAIT A SECOND," Frank said, staring down his nose at the heavy sword's lethal tip. "I can explain."

Brubaker narrowed his eyes and, with a steady hand, kept the sword trained on Frank's cranium. "All right, let's have it—and it better be good."

"Well," Frank said. He had to think quickly. "I came in to use your computer."

"My computer?"

"That's right. At practice today I noticed that my reflexes were off."

The billionare studied Frank closely. "So?"

"Well, I got worried. If I mess up, I know you'll send me home."

"What's that got to do with my computer?" Brubaker demanded.

"It's Sword Master," he said. "At home, I play it all the time. It's great for coordination and quickness. Anyway, I haven't played in days, and I figured I could use a few games to bring me up to speed."

"What made you so sure I had the game?" Brubaker asked.

"A serious fencing fan like yourself? How could you not?"

Brubaker eyed Frank. "There's still the question of how you got in."

Frank looked Brubaker straight in the eye. "I have to admit I picked the lock."

Brubaker nodded slowly. "You've got some interesting skills. I never would have pegged you for a . . ." His voice trailed off, and he finally lowered the sword. "All right. I'll take your word for it."

Frank took a step toward the door.

"Hold it right there," Brubaker said. "Before you go, let's have a little demonstration."

"You mean of Sword Master?" Frank said.

Brubaker gestured toward the desk. "Of course. Maybe I can pick up some pointers from an expert."

"As I said," Frank said, "I'm pretty rusty."

"If you play as much as you claim," Brubaker said, "you don't completely lose it in a couple of days." He moved to his desk, propped the sword against it, and bent over the keyboard, punching in a few commands. The Sword Master logo, with the title scrawled in bamboo-style letters, filled the screen.

Brubaker pulled out the desk chair, stepped aside, and nodded for Frank to sit. Frank settled in and, with Brubaker looking over his shoulder, gazed at the screen. He saw a sword slowly rotating in the middle of a green field. An army of burly opponents lined the top of the screen, while a full hourglass stood at the top right corner.

Brubaker reached over Frank's shoulder and stabbed the G key with his finger. The hourglass flipped and started to empty its sand.

"Hurry up," Brubaker said. "Time's a-wasting."

Frank raised his hands to the keyboard and stared at the unfamiliar screen. True, he had never played this particular game, but it didn't look too much different from a lot of others he knew well. Frank began manipulating the keys, quickly realizing which made his little knight in armor advance, retreat, thrust, slash, and jump straight up. His first opponent—in a Zorro cape and mask—didn't seem too tough. Each time it lunged, Frank parried successfully, making the clashing swords ring. Frank was just starting to get a feel for how to attack, when Zorro pulled a sneaky counterattack that cut Frank's knight in two. The computer groaned.

"I'm surprised you fell for that one," Brubaker said. "But you still have two knights left, you know."

In the second round, Frank racked up a fairly good score against a bearded pirate with a peg leg and a squawking parrot on his shoulder. When it was over, the high scores panel appeared, and Frank typed his initials two spaces below a top scorer whose initials were, not surprisingly, T.D.B.

In the third round, Frank pulled out all the stops, and when the high scores board appeared again, the blank space this time was at the very top. Frank typed "F.H."

"Not bad," Brubaker conceded as he flicked off the machine. He seemed genuinely impressed. "You can go now, Frank. I'm going to have the lock changed, but I'm warning you: don't even think of coming to this floor again."

"I'm sorry, Mr. Brubaker," Frank said, standing in the door. "I promise I'll never do anything like that again. It was a silly mistake. I guess I got carried away."

"Fine," Brubaker said. "Now good night."

With a half wave, half salute, Frank said, "Good night, sir," then turned and hurried back downstairs.

* * *

The next morning, Frank joined about a dozen other young fencers in the main studio for foil practice.

"All right, you know the drill: right knee is bent directly over right instep," Hedrick barked at the group. "Left knee stays straight, left foot stays flat. Weight balanced on both feet. Keep your torso erect."

Hedrick was a demanding taskmaster, constantly barking commands and correcting individual lapses. "Keep the proper separation between your feet. No ups and downs during advance or retreat. Heel touches the floor first."

This was a much tougher workout than what Frank was used to at the Bayport Salle. He was with experts now. If he hadn't been in top shape from karate, football, and basketball, he would never have been able to keep up with this group. As it was, he felt as if his fencing skills were improving by leaps and bounds.

"All right," Hedrick said, "now for some bouting. Frank, why don't you give it a try?"

"All right," Frank said, deciding to play along.

To his surprise, Hedrick handed him a samurai sword and gave Vince Beatty a battle-ax.

"Ready," Hedrick said, "and—begin."

Beatty came in swinging. Frank parried, deflecting the heavy ax with his long, curved blade, but as the weapons clashed, Frank felt pangs shoot up his wrists and arms. Frank realized his best strategy would be to dodge and duck, then rush in before Beatty regained full control of his weapon, which he was swinging like a big baseball bat.

Fighting this way, Frank held his own for about five minutes. He was getting winded, and he could sense his opponent was, too. He finally ended the session when he ducked under one particularly powerful swing that spun Beatty halfway around and jabbed his sword hilt into his opponent's ribs. Beatty straightened up at Frank's blow.

"All right—good work, gentlemen," Hedrick said, collecting their weapons. "Now, everybody gather round and listen up.

"Let's talk a little bit about the samurai," the coach began, touching the point of Frank's curved sword to the floor and resting his hands on the butt. "The more you know about them, the better.

"The samurai have a strong sense of honor—*bushido,* it's called, or 'the way of the warrior.' It dates from the Japanese feudal system and has much in common with the European code of chivalry: both stress courage, endurance, honesty, courtesy, and especially loyalty to one's ruler.

"A Japanese lord once sent his best samurai to kill an enemy. The samurai was about to be-head his victim, when the other spat in his face. The samurai was furious, but he sheathed his sword and walked away. He knew that if he killed the other at that moment, it would have been out of personal anger. Since he had been ordered to kill the other, to do so for any other reason would be to dishonor his lord; so his enemy went free." Hedrick smiled. "At least, for the time being." Hedrick surveyed his young men, who seemed impressed. "All right—shower time."

Frank went over to the fencing caddy, and as he was hanging up his damp jacket, he heard a voice behind him. "Hey, Frank."

Frank turned and saw Zach Barns.

"How's it going, Zach?" Frank said.

Barns nodded as he came over. "That was pretty decent." His voice held a new tone of respect. "Some of us seniors are skipping lunch to drive into town. Want to come?"

"Count me in," Frank said. "And thanks for the invite."

Maybe he'd be able to slip away for a few minutes and use a phone. For that matter, maybe once they were off the castle grounds, they'd be more likely to open up. Then he could find out if anyone knew anything about Adam Ross.

"Meet you in front after everybody's showered up," Barns said. "Say, twenty minutes?"

After a quick shower, Frank dressed and went out to wait in front of the castle, taking the time to check out Brubaker's sports car collection. There were four different models parked there this afternoon, two German, one Italian, one British, various colors and years, all of them convertibles with their tops down.

When the main door to the castle creaked open, five fencers came out. Frank was sorry to see Friedrich Schiller among them. Schiller didn't look too happy to see Frank, either.

"Trips to the city are usually reserved for seniors," he said. He gave Frank a long, hard look. Then, as if to show he was the one who could bend the rules if he liked, he added, "We'll make an exception this time, as long as you behave yourself, Hardy."

Schiller beckoned Frank over to one of the cars, a four-year-old mid-engine two-seater that, if Frank's memory served him well, had a turbo-charged 350-horsepower engine and a top speed of about 190 miles per hour.

"Hardy, you're driving with me," Schiller said.

The road to town wound over scenic hills, through forests, and past farmland with well-kept vineyards.

Schiller led the way, with the other drivers working to keep up. As soon as they left the castle grounds and were through the main gate, Schiller jammed a heavy metal CD into the player and cranked up the volume. He didn't say a word, and he drove very fast.

Schiller took a few hairpin turns at high speed, braking into them, then accelerating out. The car's rear end fishtailed, and its tires squealed. Frank knew this wasn't skilled driving; it was just showing off.

On one of the first straightaways, Schiller passed two cars, then stayed in the oncoming lane for several extra seconds, playing chicken with a truck, which blared its horn and flashed its headlights as the sports car swerved back into its lane just in time to avoid a head-on collision.

Frank noticed the speedometer at close to 200 kilometers an hour—about 120 miles per hour—as they completed the pass. He looked over at the senior fencer, who was squinting into the distance with the trace of a smug little smile on his face, and had to shake his head. He would have loved a chance to show this jerk some real driving skills.

When they reached the city, Schiller announced, "We'll park in the old section and walk over to the new. It's just across the bridge."

The old section, on the south side of the river, had narrow cobblestone streets lined with all kinds of shops. There were sidewalk cafés and several large open squares that reminded Frank of those in some other European cities he'd visited.

Schiller led the little group of fencers on a shopping spree in the newer section of the city, with its blacktopped streets, modern buildings, and fast-food eateries. They went to a record mart, a sporting goods store, and an electronics shop. Frank estimated that the five other fencers charged between $1,000 and $1,500 worth of goods in less than an hour. As they left the electronics shop, Frank noticed a pharmacy, a butcher shop, a grocery store, and a telegraph office. He was still looking for a chance to make his phone call.

"We probably should get back soon," DeMarco said, checking his watch.

"Take it easy for once," Schiller said. "We've got one more stop." He led the group around the corner to a pizza parlor.

While they were waiting, Schiller puffed out his chest to show off the heavy metal sweatshirt he'd just bought. "Hey, is this bad or what?" It was fluorescent yellow, with white skulls and flaming arrows leaping out of a guitar. "The last one they had, too."

At the counter, everyone ordered slices to go. Frank ordered one with extra sauce and double the anchovies. As they walked around the corner to find a place to sit in the square, Schiller asked Frank, "Got enough fish there, Hardy?"

"I think so," Frank said. And with that, he stepped off the curb into the path of an oncoming car. It honked loudly, and Frank said, "Whoa," then jumped back, making sure that his greasy slice flew right onto Schiller's new sweatshirt.

"Ach!" Schiller shouted. He leaned forward and plucked it away from him so the mess wouldn't soak through. "Hardy, I ought to kill you."

"Better just put some water on it," DeMarco said. "That grease'll stain."

Flinging his own slice onto the street, Schiller growled, "I'll be back," and stalked off.

Frank looked at his ruined lunch on the ground. "Guys, I'm going back for another slice."

Frank turned the corner and rushed past the pizza shop into the grocery store. Sure enough, it had a pay phone. He called the international operator and asked to place a collect call to the United States. He checked his watch. Bayport was six hours behind Heidelberg, which would make it seven-thirty A.M. at home. Breakfast time. After about twenty seconds, the operator came back on. "I'm sorry, sir, but the line's busy. May I suggest you try again later?" He decided the telegraph office was a better bet, hung up, and hurried over there.

Behind a counter covered with posters that

explained the rates, a short, bald man of about sixty looked up from a newspaper.

"Uh, hi," Frank said. "Do you speak English?"

The man nodded and smiled. "Ahh . . . English . . . ja. Good English."

"I want to send a telegram to the United States," Frank said. "Can I send it collect? Is that possible?"

"Sure, sure, but you know they must accept." The man nodded agreeably. He gave Frank a small pad of carbon-backed forms and a pen. "You write here."

Leaning on the counter, Frank quickly jotted his message, filled in the address and phone number, and handed it back. "One moment for confirmation, sir," the man said, handing the original to a technician at a keyboard and a copy back to Frank.

Frank heard a commotion outside, then looked up and saw Friedrich Schiller pull open the door and come striding in. He wasn't smiling.

Chapter 12

"WHATS GOING ON, HARDY?" Schiller said, confronting Frank with the others flanking him on either side.

Frank knew there was no point in lying, and he'd set it up so he didn't have to. "I was sending a telegram," he said.

Schiller bared his teeth in a half smile. "You know the rules," he said, glancing quickly at the manager behind the counter. "Now, let's get out of here."

On the sidewalk, all five fencers crowded around Frank.

"Okay," Schiller demanded. "What were you saying—and to whom?"

Frank held the crinkled carbon to Schiller's face. "Here's a copy. Read it yourself."

Schiller snatched the slip away, held it up, and read aloud. " 'Dear Grandma Jo. Best wishes on your 90th birthday. Hope the operation doesn't leave a scar. Love, Frank.' "

"Satisfied?" Frank asked.

Schiller eyed Frank suspiciously. "Birthday wishes to your grandmother? What's this about an operation?"

"Just a family joke," Frank said. "My grandmother thinks her nose is too big. My mother always said that when she turned ninety, she'll pay for a nose job as a present." Frank shrugged. "I figured what's the harm in sending a message to my grandma?"

Schiller studied Frank and Frank couldn't tell whether the older student believed him or not.

"You know all contact with outsiders is forbidden," Schiller said at last. "I'll be reporting this to Coach Hedrick." He pocketed the note and turned to the others. "All right, we've wasted enough time—let's get back to the castle."

Meanwhile, Joe and Coach Kupcek were arriving in Heidelberg, weary after the all-night flight from the States and a fifty-mile train ride from the Frankfurt airport.

"Where to, Joe?" Kupcek asked as they made their way through the station.

"We start with this," Joe said, handing the

coach the scrap of paper with Hans Hedrick's address written on it. They hailed a cab, and Kupcek read the address to the driver. He nodded and sped off through town. Joe was surprised at how fast the cabbies—and everyone else—drove, but they did all seem to be efficient and courteous drivers. After about ten minutes, they pulled up to a large house with a metal gate in a quiet, well-to-do neighborhood.

"This must be it," Joe said. He led Kupcek through the gate and up the steps of the front porch and clanged the door knocker. After a few moments, a tall, ruggedly built young man appeared. At his side were two huge Dobermans, who stared at Joe and Kupcek, their cropped ears standing straight up.

"We're looking for Hans Hedrick," Kupcek said.

"Herr Hedrick isn't home." The young man spoke in a flat tone.

"Any idea when he's expected back?" Joe asked.

"Herr Hedrick doesn't report to me," he said. "If you would state your names and the nature of your business, I could give him a message."

"If you'd mention we—" Kupcek began.

"Forget it," Joe said quickly. "We're just old fencing buddies, and we'll try again later. Thanks." Joe took the coach's arm, and they left.

"We don't want to lose the element of surprise," Joe said as they let themselves out the gate. "Let's see if we can track him down through some of the local fencing clubs."

"I know a few," Kupcek said. They found a café about five blocks away on a boulevard, and the coach used the pay phone there while Joe had a fresh orange juice and a delicious almond pastry.

"Well, here's the good news," Kupcek said, joining Joe at his table a few minutes later. "There's a small meet scheduled this afternoon at two. This being the fencing capital, there's always plenty of action, mostly among local competitors. This one's at the Heidelberg Fencing Academy—not far."

"With any luck, Hedrick'll be hanging around, probably trying to recruit fencers away from other coaches," Joe said. "Meantime, we have a few hours. Let's go find a hotel and get some rest."

They took a cab back to the train station and checked into the Hotel Metropole right across the square for a two-hour nap, followed by a quick lunch.

The Heidelberg Fencing Academy was a short bus ride from the hotel, and Joe and Coach Kupcek arrived about twenty minutes early for the matches. The academy was housed in an ornately carved, distinguished-looking gray stone building that looked as if it had been a palace in an earlier era.

"Keep an eye out for Hedrick," Joe said as he and the coach entered the hall. "We don't want you to lose any more buttons."

They were directed to a large, airy gymnasium, where fencers were warming up and spectators were taking their seats on several dozen metal folding chairs. Joe saw a few he recognized from New York. This was a very similar scene, only smaller.

Then Joe spotted the man he and Coach Kupcek had traveled thousands of miles to find, standing on the far side of the room. Wearing white fencing trousers and a short jacket, he was demonstrating an épée move to a young fencer.

"Bingo," Joe said, nodding in that direction.

Kupcek followed Joe's gaze and spotted Hedrick. "Should we talk to him now?" he asked.

"Absolutely," Joe said. "I want to see his reaction when he recognizes me."

Joe and the coach made their way across the room, sneaking up behind Hedrick. When he was at his elbow, Joe leaned close and practically shouted, "Well, hello, Coach Hedrick!"

Hedrick turned and he took a step back, and his face went pale.

"Surprised to see us?" Joe asked.

Hedrick cleared his throat and paused to regain his composure. "You could say that, yes."

Looking at his old rival Kupcek, Hedrick added, "So, what brings you two to Heidelberg?"

"My brother," Joe said.

"Ah, yes, of course. He's got some talent. Has he come to compete?" Hedrick made a show of peering around the room.

Joe narrowed his eyes. Two could play this game.

"Actually," Joe said, "I haven't heard from Frank since Saturday night."

"Sounds irresponsible of him."

"He called in a big hurry," Joe said, "and just before the line went dead, he said he was with you. Now, how do you explain that?"

Hedrick shrugged. "Maybe you misheard him, or he was confused—"

"I know what I heard," Joe said.

"Well, unless you can prove I saw your brother since New York, that is just a lot of hot air. Excuse me. I have a team to prepare." He turned and walked away.

"I'd say he was pretty nervous," Joe said. "He definitely knows something. We can work on him some more later. For now, is there anybody else you know from the circuit?"

"A fair number," Laslo said, scanning the crowd. Sure enough, moments later he said, "Ah, there's Pete Ronson." Joe saw a man in his fifties, of medium height. Though his hair was gray and thinning, he looked strong as he practiced lunges near one of the strips.

"Pete's a nice guy, but sort of nosy," Kupcek said. "If anyone minds other people's business, he does."

When Ronson saw Kupcek, he waved and came over. The two exchanged hearty greetings.

"Pete, I'd like you to meet Joe Hardy," Coach Kupcek said. "Joe—Pete Ronson."

As Joe shook his hand, Ronson eyed Joe closely. "So, what brings you to Heidelberg, Joe? Are you competing?"

"Actually, I'm not," Joe replied. "I'm looking for somebody. Would you mind if I ask you some questions?"

"Fire away," Ronson said agreeably. "Just let me get a sip of water here first." He filled a plastic cup from his pitcher. "People don't realize how hot fencing can make you, but just try doing heavy exercise with three layers of clothing, a mask over your head, and a thick, padded leather glove." He took a long drink.

"Saturday night," Joe began, "my brother, Frank, disappeared from Bayport after a big fencing meet in New York City." Joe went on to describe Hedrick's blatant attempts to recruit Adam Ross, Ross's quick exit and disappearance, and Frank's phone call. "Obviously, Hedrick has something to do with it, but when I spoke to him just now, he denied it. Do you know much about the man—why he's so secretive?"

"I know I find him utterly contemptible," Ronson said. He crushed the empty cup and flung it into a trash basket. "A number of other folks on the circuit feel the same way."

Ronson turned toward Hedrick, who stood across the room with a small group of young fencers. Joe was surprised to see Hedrick staring directly across at them. His expression was hard to read. He clearly wasn't smiling, but he wasn't frowning, either. Then he quickly turned away.

"He doesn't look too thrilled to see us talking," Joe observed.

"Only one thing thrills him," Ronson said, "and that's winning, at any cost, for the greater glory of Hans Hedrick. I've seen him send injured fencers onto the strip. The judges stopped it, but Hedrick didn't give a hoot if they got hurt worse."

"What else do you know about him?" Joe asked. "I take it he lives nearby?"

"Everything's always hush-hush with him, but I've heard he occasionally works up on the hill."

"The hill?"

"The castle. T. D. Brubaker's place—didn't you know? He has a team that competes sometimes down here. Hedrick works with them, though why he wastes his time with a second-rate group like that, I don't know. They're okay—just not top caliber. I guess even money can't buy you talent, can it?"

The public address system blared an announcement in German followed by an English translation: "Attention, fencers in the first bouts, please take your places on the strips."

"That's me," Ronson said. "I'll talk more later if you like."

The older fencer stepped to one end of the strip where an official helped him "wire up," clipping a retractable wire that ran from the scoreboard to a short lead dangling from the back of his jacket. As was the case in foil, the swordplay was so fast in épée that the bouts were scored electronically. In foil, the fair target was only the opponent's torso, but with épée, it included any part of the body at all—even the feet and toes. Since a foot attack could be hard to spot, the strip was copper-coated for the épée bouts; if a blade tip touched the metal, the completed circuit registered a miss.

Joe and Laslo took seats near the sidelines to watch. As Ronson neared the mat, he stooped to adjust his left pant leg. Joe saw the tip of his épée brush the strip and a spark erupt at the point of contact. That didn't seem right. Come to think of it, it made no sense. The current running through there was supposed to be minute, nowhere near strong enough to cause a spark like that.

Joe got up to warn Ronson, who was stepping onto the strip. But as soon as the fencer's foot touched the copper surface, he jerked spasmodically upright, his back arching and his masked head whipping back.

Chapter 13

JOE JUMPED up from his seat, snatched Ronson's pitcher, and flung its contents at the scoring transformer. It immediately crackled, popped, and sent out a shower of sparks. The room's lights dimmed momentarily as the transformer short-circuited, then the machine went dead.

Joe and Coach Kupcek rushed to Ronson, who had collapsed on the strip.

"Hey, Pete," Coach Kupcek said, carefully removing his friend's mask. "Can you hear me?"

Ronson's eyes were open, but he was completely dazed. As the crowd quickly gathered around, a man identifying himself as the fencing academy's doctor cleared a path so he could examine the patient.

"You saved his life," a woman said to Joe. "How did you know to throw water? I would have thought it would shock him worse."

Joe shook his head. "Electricity takes the path of least resistance. The water created a more direct route for the current than traveling through Ronson—so direct, in fact, it shorted out at the source."

"Nice work, kid," she said. "You deserve a medal or something."

Within minutes, two ambulance attendants wheeled in a gurney and carefully lifted the fallen fencer onto it. Kupcek got word about which hospital they'd be taking him to so he could check on him later.

"I hope he's going to be all right," Joe said.

"Me, too. I guess he can't tell us any more about Hedrick now, though," Kupcek said.

"Does this sort of thing happen often?" Joe said.

"I've never seen it before," Coach Kupcek said. "In the 'sixties, an Olympic fencer was actually electrocuted during the games. He was soaked with sweat and still wired up. He sat on a metal chair whose front legs happened to be on the metal strip. I thought they changed the design of the transformers after that so it couldn't happen again."

"Hmmm," Joe said, turning to examine the TV-size electrical unit. It was still dripping water, and there was a puddle on the floor beneath it. Joe detected a burnt smell. He crouched on his heels to take a closer look.

"Careful," Kupcek warned.

"Don't worry, it's shorted out," Joe said, but just to be sure, he pulled the plug. "Okay, here's the wire to Ronson's line. And it looks like someone connected a wire across these two screws. That reroutes the current from the wall directly to Ronson's line, bypassing the step-down coil so the voltage to his sword is full-strength."

"Sabotage?"

"Definitely," Joe said. "Somebody just zapped Pete Ronson."

"Maybe that somebody saw him talking to us and wanted to put a stop to it," Coach Kupcek said.

"My thoughts exactly," Joe replied. He straightened up and looked over to where Hans Hedrick was absorbed in giving instructions to one of his students.

Frank was dripping sweat as he opened his locker and took out a towel. He was in the Castle Salle locker room, ready to shower following his afternoon workout. Carlos DeMarco walked in and set down his mask and sword; the others would be joining them soon.

"Nervous about tonight?" Frank asked.

DeMarco turned. "What do you mean?"

"The bout. The match. I'm wondering if you're nervous."

DeMarco mumbled something Frank didn't hear.

Frank picked up his towel. "If you're still afraid to talk—"

"You know, according to the rules . . ." DeMarco said.

"Carlos, you can bend the rules a little," Frank said. "Otherwise, I'm going to wind up getting kicked out of here."

"What do you mean?"

"I keep getting in trouble. Schiller obviously has it in for me, and this afternoon with the telegram sure didn't help. Yesterday Brubaker caught me someplace I wasn't supposed to be—"

"What do you mean someplace you weren't supposed to be?" DeMarco asked.

"Up on the third floor," Frank said.

"That's strictly off limits," DeMarco replied. "Mr. Brubaker's office is up there. The only other thing is a supply closet."

"Whatever," Frank said. "I'm telling you, I'm worried they're going to send me home."

"Why don't you talk to Coach Hedrick or Mr. Brubaker?"

"I would," Frank said, "but they're always busy, and I don't really feel comfortable interrupting them. Couldn't you just fill me in on a few things? Help me keep out of trouble?"

Again, DeMarco hesitated.

"Okay, Carlos," Frank said. "The truth is, I'm looking for some information. A year and a half ago, my cousin disappeared. Nobody in the family has heard a word from him. Can't you help me?"

"Wow," DeMarco said. "What was his name?"

"Jake McCleary," Frank said without missing a beat.

"I never heard of him," DeMarco said.

"His family just wants to know where he went," Frank said. "Help me out, and I promise this conversation stays between us." He held out his hand. DeMarco paused, looked Frank in the eye, then reached out and shook his hand.

"Thanks," Frank said. "I owe you one. So what's the story? How long have you been at the castle?"

"Not long. About four months. Most of the others have been here longer—especially Schiller. But no one knows exactly. Like I said, we don't talk about it."

"How'd you wind up here?" Frank asked.

"I was at a tournament in Philadelphia, and Coach Hedrick talked to me afterward. Castle Salle sounded great. I'd been living with my aunt on and off since my parents died when I was little, and it seemed like a good deal."

"Have you fought many bouts?"

"Ten or twelve." DeMarco rubbed his forearm, where Frank noticed a jagged scar. "I've had a few close calls."

"Has anyone ever tried to leave?" Frank asked.

"Well, I know a few who aren't around anymore," DeMarco said. "But I don't know what happened to them. Mr. Brubaker said they went home. I'll tell you this, it looked like one fencer got killed about two months ago. Not everybody saw it, but I know he got stabbed, and it was bad. They hustled him out of there. Mr. Brubaker said he'd be okay and he might come back from the hospital. We haven't seen him yet."

"Well, why don't you all leave? Don't you want to get out of here?"

"Frank, you heard it from Mr. Brubaker and Coach Hedrick. We're the best in the world. We're champions. We've got an awesome lifestyle. Wouldn't you rather be doing this than doing homework every night and working some crummy after-school job, bagging groceries or cooking greasy french fries?"

"Okay, you've got a point there," Frank said. "So tell me more about tonight. Who's in the audience? Just rich people who're bored with the racetrack?"

"Well, they *are* rich," DeMarco said. "I hear a lot of them are corporate bigwigs—C.E.O.s, presidents."

"That would explain all the secrecy," Frank said. "It wouldn't exactly be good public relations for stockholders to find out supposedly responsible, level-headed corporate executives were betting on no-holds-barred bloodbaths." Frank looked hard at DeMarco. "You know, there's still the question of Adam Ross."

DeMarco didn't answer.

"Come on, Carlos, don't hold back," Frank said.

"All right—yes. He *was* here, but just for part of the day before you arrived. When he got here, he flipped during his first practice match," DeMarco said.

"What do you mean, *'flipped'?"*

"Someone got hurt on the strip near his—not even that badly—and Ross just froze and couldn't fence. It was the sight of blood, I guess. Anyway, he was sent home. Brubaker and Hedrick weren't even here yet before he was sent packing."

"He was sent home?" Frank said. "How do you know?"

"Coach Hedrick told us when he arrived with

you," DeMarco said. "He said Adam didn't work out, so they sent him home."

Frank knew there wasn't much chance of that with all he'd seen.

"Tell me something else," Frank said, "What was that business about samurai in Hedrick's lecture this morning?"

Just then the locker room door opened, and several more fencers came in, including Friedrich Schiller. DeMarco shot Frank a worried look; Frank just nodded slightly and turned to his locker.

"So, any word from Grandma yet?" Schiller said.

"Do me a favor, Schiller, grow up," Frank said. This turned a few heads.

Schiller's eyes flashed angrily. "We don't need any wimps around here, Hardy, just men."

"Now, that's something you would know about—being a wimp," Frank said. He'd had enough of Schiller's bullying.

One or two of the others smiled, a fact Schiller couldn't have missed.

"You shouldn't even be here," Schiller said. "All you do is start trouble. You've got an attitude problem, and I'm going to do something about it." With that, Schiller tugged off his glove and whipped it smartly across Frank's jaw.

The blow didn't hurt, but Frank understood

what it meant. Schiller was challenging him to a duel.

With the sound of the glove slap still echoing off the lockers, Frank reared back and punched Schiller in the jaw, connecting solidly. Schiller staggered backward, stumbling against one of the metal doors.

"I won't fence you," Frank said, "but smack me again, and I'll give you plenty more of that."

Schiller jumped to his feet, his eyes bulging. "All right," he said, reaching into his open locker and whipping out a saber. Brandishing the gleaming blade, he said, "I'm going to give you a permanent souvenir of your stay here. You know what a Heidelberg scar is?" Schiller spun toward the others. "Hold him down."

Frank's adrenaline surged. He whipped around toward the other fencers, bracing for their attack. He knew he might fight off two or three, but against all six—including Schiller—his chances would be slim.

But then Frank saw the others hesitate.

"Hold it, Friedrich," DeMarco said. "Six against one? I don't know. . . ."

"You idiots. I said grab him!" Schiller shouted.

But the others hung back, exchanging glances. No one wanted to be the first to gang up on a teammate.

"They've got no reason to listen to you,"

Frank said. "Do you think they're your personal army or something?"

"Grab him *now!*" Schiller shouted again.

But the others stood firm.

"Looks like you're on your own," Frank said.

Schiller cocked his sword arm and screamed at Frank, "I'll make you pay for this!" then charged, swinging the big weapon recklessly.

Chapter 14

FRANK SNATCHED A TOWEL from the bench and snapped it in Schiller's face. Then he unleashed a powerful spinning-wheel karate kick that caught his attacker on the chin. Schiller's head snapped sideways and whacked hard against a metal locker. He dropped his saber and slithered limply to the floor.

The other fencers stared.

"Nice move, Frank," Barns said.

"*Now* would someone tell me exactly what's going on around here?" Frank asked.

The fencers exchanged looks, then DeMarco finally spoke up. "Frank, it's as you probably guessed. We use live blades during the bouts. Sure, it's dangerous, but it's not as brutal as you might think. It's always stopped at first blood."

Frank was familiar with the concept. In fact, it was why fencers wore white. If a duel was agreed to end at "first cut," it made the blood easy to detect and confirm the winner.

"First blood or not, it sounds like at least one person's dead," Frank said, "and probably plenty more."

"Okay, maybe there were a few accidents where the ref didn't stop the bout soon enough," DeMarco said. "I'm not saying this is completely safe, but it isn't kill or be killed."

"No?" Frank said. "I think that's exactly what it is. Can't you see? Why do you think everything's such a big secret? Why aren't you allowed any outside contact?"

"They're protecting us," Barns said. "Fencing at this level, we can't afford the distractions."

"Come on, they're not protecting you, they're using you," Frank said. "Brubaker's got you brainwashed. He tells you you're great and buys you fancy toys so you won't see this place for what it is—a suicide camp."

Nobody said anything, so Frank pressed on. "What happens to the guys who get hurt? Why don't you ever see them again? Where is Broussard? Was he killed? I think he was. And why can't you ever go up to the third floor? What's up there that Brubaker doesn't want you to see? And for that matter, what happened to Adam

Ross? All he did was have a normal reaction to a bloody, gory fight."

"Mr. Brubaker sent him home," Barns said.

"You believe that?" Frank scoffed. He knew he was going out on a limb, but he had their attention now. "You know what? I think Brubaker had him killed."

"What?" several fencers responded.

"Brubaker would never let him go," Frank said. "Not once he saw what goes on here. The same's true for all of you. Brubaker is setting you up to die. Just so his pals can do some high-stakes wagering."

The fencers exchanged looks.

"You heard the man's speech at dinner," Frank continued. "To him you're not human beings. You're just 'natural resources.' "

There was another pause.

"What Frank's saying does make some sense," DeMarco said to his teammates. "We're all so caught up in this lifestyle, we've been ignoring the reality. Frank, you asked about the samurai. Well, we're supposed to fight a group of them tonight."

"What else do you know about it?" Frank asked.

"Brubaker and Hedrick have been building up to this for weeks," Beatty said. "The ultimate bout."

Frank nodded slowly. "I don't care how good

you guys are. This is going to be a slaughter. Samurai fighters don't go for first blood—they go for the kill."

"Brubaker can't make us fight if we don't want to," Beatty said.

"He's smart, he's powerful, and so far he's been calling all the shots," Frank said. "I think some of you guys are ready to make a move, but you haven't been able to admit it yet. Once word gets out, Brubaker's death bouts are history, and he and Hedrick go to jail. What do you say we make a break for it? Are you with me?"

"I could be," DeMarco said.

"Same here," Barns said.

"And here," Beatty said.

Everyone was so focused on Frank's speech, they hadn't noticed Schiller stirring. Suddenly, he jumped to his feet and bolted for the stairway.

"Stop him!" Frank shouted. He raced after the senior fencer, but Schiller made it to the second floor and slammed the door before Frank was halfway up. Frank tried the knob, leaned into the door with his shoulder, then gave it a solid kick, but it wouldn't budge.

"He jammed something against it," Frank said. "I'm sure he's on his way to warn Brubaker."

"We'd better get out of here," Barns said. "We don't have much time."

"Wait a second," Frank said. "Remember Brubaker said he never wasted a resource, that if he couldn't use it right away, he'd save it for later? I think he might have been talking about Adam Ross."

"You said he killed Ross," DeMarco said.

"I had to say *something* to open your eyes," Frank said. "I think I know where Ross might be. Go down and tell the rest of them to wait. Give me five minutes, then head out to the cars. You know where the keys are—on those hooks in the back hall.

"Just remember—everyone in front in five minutes, no sooner." Frank checked his watch. "I've got six-sixteen. See you in five."

Meanwhile, Joe and Coach Kupcek had been sitting in a café, finishing up a light supper.

"I feel like we're stumped," Kupcek said.

"Not yet," Joe said. "I'm going to call home to see if Frank checked in." He used a phone booth in back to place a collect call to Bayport.

Laura Hardy accepted the call right away. "Joe, where are you?" she said.

"Mom, something came up. I can't explain right now. Have you heard from Frank?"

"Have I ever—Joe, I wish you would clue

me in. He sent a telegram from Heidelberg, Germany."

"From Heidelberg? Great. What's it say?"

Laura read the message, and Joe jotted it down.

"Joe, what's this about Grandma Jo's ninetieth birthday and an operation and a scar?"

"Mom, I promise I'll explain later. As soon as I figure it out myself. Now I've got to go. 'Bye."

He hung up and went back to tell Kupcek about the message.

"So what does it mean?" the coach asked.

Joe flattened the paper on the table. "It's a coded message, which means either he can't or he doesn't want to let anybody know he's contacting us. 'Dear Grandma Jo'—that's me."

" 'Best wishes on your ninetieth birthday'?" Kupcek asked.

Joe pondered that one. "Ninety or nine. Could be an address, but there's no street. Does the number mean anything in fencing?"

"Not that I can think of," the coach said.

"Okay," Joe continued. " 'Here's hoping the operation doesn't leave a scar.' What about the word *operation?* Any special meaning in fencing?"

Kupcek furrowed his brow. "No, but there's the Heidelberg scar, of course."

"What's that?" Joe asked.

The coach told Joe about the infamous mark.

"So it's right around the cheekbone?" Joe said. "You know, T. D. Brubaker has a scar just like that. I noticed it the second day of the tournament. Before he almost got electrocuted, Pete Ronson was telling us about Brubaker's castle and how Hedrick works for him. Frank's call and this telegram . . . Brubaker's scar . . . Hedrick's work at the castle. It's all coming together. Funny how Frank got the chloroform in his mask after we asked Hedrick about Adam Ross, then Ronson got sapped after he told us about the Brubaker-Hedrick connection. I say we go up to that castle and check it out."

"Are you saying maybe Frank is being held prisoner up there?" Kupcek said. "And Adam, too?"

"That's exactly what I'm saying," Joe said. "And there's only one way to find out. Let's go."

When Frank got to the third floor, he eased the door open and peered down the hallway. There was no sign of Schiller, which could mean he was already there waiting in ambush.

Frank crept toward the storage closet. He tried the handle, but the door was locked. He glanced back toward the stairs, then knocked three times. No answer. He tried again, harder, and this time he heard three muffled thumps in reply. There was somebody in there.

He was about to rattle the handle again when he heard footsteps in the stairway. He quickly slipped into the alcove behind the suit of armor as Friedrich Schiller came flying up the stairs and raced past him toward Brubaker's office. He thought about tackling him, but whoever was inside the office would hear the scuffle.

Schiller flung open Brubaker's door and said, "Sir, it's an emergency." Then he told Brubaker what had happened in the locker room.

"This is serious," Brubaker said.

Frank heard another voice. "Sounds like we've got a mutiny on our hands." It was Hedrick.

"What a shame you can't control your fencers better," said a third voice in what sounded like an Asian accent. "This would never happen in Japan."

"Maybe not," Brubaker said, "but we have to deal with the situation. Mr. Nikumi, may I suggest we start our tournament a little early?"

There was silence. Then the guest said, "Since it seems we don't have a choice, I agree."

There was a rustle of chairs, and Frank quickly ducked back into the shadows as a group of five filed into the hall. There was Brubaker, Hedrick, Schiller, and an older man in a suit and aviator glasses, no doubt Mr. Nikumi. The fifth man was about six-foot-four and a solid two-eighty. Barefoot, in a loose-fitting black samurai *ghi* with a long-handled sword hanging from a thick black belt at his waist, he cut an imposing figure.

"Where are your fighters, Gosaki?" Nikumi asked, speaking English probably for Brubaker and Hedrick's benefit.

"In their rooms," replied the huge man. "Awaiting orders."

"Take them to the locker room," Nikumi said. "Engage the young men down there. Be sure they do not get out."

The samurai bowed his head. "Yes, sir."

Frank waited for the group to go downstairs, then he went back to check the storage room door. It had a heavy, old-fashioned lock, too much for his paper clip. The keyhole was huge, and the key for it wouldn't be anything Brubaker could carry on a ring in his pocket. Then Frank remembered the antique paperweight on Brubaker's desk. He had a hunch it would open this door.

Frank went over to Brubaker's office door and saw he had made good on his promise to change the cylinder. Frank stepped back and uncoiled a powerful front kick. *Whump.* The door trembled but held. Frank's leg muscles were hard from all the fencing he'd done in the past few months. He braced himself and kicked again; this time, there was a splintering sound. On the third kick, wood pieces flew, and the door crashed in.

Frank rushed in and flicked on the desk lamp. The key wasn't on the desk. He tried the top drawer, but it was locked. He snatched a dagger off the wall and forced the drawer open, but it was full of folders. He forced a second drawer, then a third, where he finally found the big key. Knowing every second counted, he snatched it up and spun around—to find T. D. Brubaker and Hans Hedrick standing in the doorway.

"Back for some more computer games?" Brubaker asked.

Frank clutched the key in his fist as he stared at the saber in Hedrick's hand.

"Good thing we came back to check the office," Brubaker said.

"You've got Adam Ross in the storage room, don't you?" Frank said.

"Why would you think that?" Brubaker asked as the two men stepped into the room.

"You told everybody he was sent home, but that was a lie. You couldn't risk his telling people about your operation. As first I thought you killed him—just dumped him out of your jet over the ocean. But last night, you made that little speech about hating waste and never destroying a valuable resource. So I realized you wouldn't just waste Adam. Not if you could get him to fight to the death so you and your millionaire friends could bet on it."

"Coach Hedrick said you were clever, Frank,

and he was right," Brubaker said. "Yes, Ross saw someone get hurt and lost his nerve. I was told he crumbled. He wouldn't fight and tried to escape. It's happened before. He was confined. We probably should have wasted him, as you put it. It would have been neater."

"Well, it's all over now," Frank said. "The fencers know everything, and none of them will fight anymore."

"You're wrong there, Frank. They'll fight, all right, because they'll be fighting for their lives against the samurai." He looked at his watch. "In fact, they should be at it any minute now . . ."

"Out of my way, Brubaker," Frank said, and took a step toward the door.

The two men stood firm. "You're not going anywhere," Brubaker said. Then, noticing the open desk drawers, he said, "And I'll take that key."

"No, you won't," Frank shot back.

Brubaker lifted the corners of his mouth in a tight smile. "Have it your way, then. He's all yours, Hans." Brubaker stepped aside, and Hedrick assumed the ready position, aiming his heavy saber at Frank, who knew that even with his martial arts training, he didn't stand a chance unarmed against a swordsman of this caliber.

Chapter 15

"STOP RIGHT THERE."

Joe Hardy's commanding voice filled the room. They all turned to see Joe and Coach Kupcek standing in the doorway, a saber in the older man's right hand.

"It's over, Brubaker," Joe said. "Your secret's out—time to call it quits."

"Not so fast," Brubaker said, and he reached for a battle sword that was hanging on the wall.

Hedrick charged with his saber, but Kupcek raised his weapon and parried the attack cleanly.

"Joe," Frank said. "I'm not even going to ask how you got in because I've got to warn the rest of them about the samurai attack. You handle things here."

Joe rushed in behind Kupcek, snatched a rapier off the wall, and said, "Take this," tossing it to his brother. Frank caught it in midair, ducked past the two coaches, and darted out the door. Joe grabbed a club off the wall to use against Brubaker as Frank raced down the hallway and leaned into the closet door.

"Adam, are you in there? Can you hear me?" Frank pounded his sword hilt on the door as he thrust the key into the lock. "It's me, Frank Hardy," Frank called. "I'm coming in." As he turned the key, he heard a voice behind him at the stairway door: "Don't count on it."

Frank turned and faced Friedrich Schiller, who was closing in on him with an épée. "I've been waiting for this chance," Schiller said.

"Schiller, this is no time for your stupid rivalry," Frank said. "The samurai are out to kill everyone."

"Not everyone," the older fencer said. "You're mine." Schiller raised his sword to touch its pommel to his lips. Then, whipping the blade down in a classic salute, he shouted, "Defend yourself!" and charged.

Frank parried just in time. They traded quick, clanging blows, and Frank held his own, but he knew he wouldn't last long against Schiller's superior experience.

Frank kept up his defense, gradually backing toward the door. He waited for an especially vicious attack, then let his sword slip, as if Schiller had knocked it out of his hand. It clanged to the stone floor. Schiller took the bait and charged, thrusting directly at Frank's heart. Frank jumped aside at the last instant. Schiller's blade nicked Frank's shirt, then buried itself a full inch into the heavy wooden door with a solid *thwack.*

Before Schiller could dislodge the sword tip, Frank shot out his fist, landing a solid left hook to his jaw. Frank followed with a right uppercut to the chin, and Schiller was out cold before he hit the stone floor. He might be a great fencer, Frank thought, but he wasn't much of a boxer.

Frank turned the key and swung the heavy door open. In the glow of a single wall torch, Frank saw a small dungeon with a tiny barred window. There was a cot, a sink, and a bucket. Adam Ross lay on top of the cot, squinting up miserably at Frank. His hands and feet were bound to the metal frame with leather straps, and his mouth was gagged. When he saw Frank, his eyes grew large.

Frank unbuckled the straps and untied the gag.

"Frank? Frank Hardy?" Ross said, his voice cracking. "What are you doing here?"

"Come on, Adam," Frank ordered. "We've got to warn everybody—if it's not too late already. Can you walk?"

"Yeah—I'm okay." Ross stood shakily and rubbed his wrists. "How did you get here? Where are Brubaker and Hedrick?"

"No time to explain now. There's a bunch of samurai fighters about to ambush the Castle team."

As they left, Frank grabbed Schiller's sword, still quivering in the door, and worked it free. He gave it to Ross, and the two raced down to the locker room.

Joe and Coach Kupcek had their hands full.

"So, one more duel . . . just like the old days," Hedrick said, grimacing at his old rival. "Except this one's to the death." He paused and then charged. Kupcek executed a classic parry, whirled his blade in a 180-degree arc, and slashed at Hedrick.

Joe eyed Brubaker, who was half crouched behind his desk, holding his big battle sword at the ready. Joe hunched forward like a middle linebacker and plowed into the desk, hoping to pin Brubaker. An open drawer caught the billionaire's knee, and he yelped in pain as he went down in a heap. Joe snatched a pair of manacles from the wall and quickly cuffed Brubaker's wrists to a heavy chair, then turned to the two coaches.

Their thrusts and parries were a blur, their blades flashing silver. Joe picked up his club, waited for his chance, then stepped in and whacked Hedrick in the midsection, knocking him out and putting a quick end to the duel.

Frank burst through the locker room door and shouted, "Quick—everybody get your swords."

"Frank, we were just getting ready to leave," DeMarco said as they all stood and stared.

"Hurry up, there's going to be a surprise attack," Frank said. "The samurai."

DeMarco, Barns, Beatty, and the rest of the Castle Salle team scrambled for their blades—just as the doors burst open and Gosaki charged in leading his band of samurai.

"Eee-*yaah!*" the Japanese fighters screamed, as they poured in with upraised swords. Within seconds it was pandemonium.

Zach Barns, wielding a saber, traded blows with a small, compactly built samurai wearing a black mask across the bottom of his face. The samurai let out shrill, bloodcurdling shrieks with each attack. Vince Beatty, who had snatched up his foil, was fighting a tall samurai who dodged acrobatically. DeMarco wielded a saber against Gosaki himself; the huge samurai warrior's combination of power and quickness made it clear why he was their leader.

The samurai swordsmen and the young fencers went at it with all they had, filling the room with the clang of clashing swords, the loud *thunks* of blades striking lockers, the furious shouts, the pained grunts, and the slap of bare feet on the floor.

Frank was pitted against a muscular samurai who leaped high and came down with killer attacks. The samurai finally launched such a powerful swipe that it cracked a bench, but it also left him open for an instant. With split-second timing, Frank fired a karate kick to his foe's solar plexus, knocking the wind out of him and taking him out of the battle.

Frank looked up and realized that the Castle team was in trouble. DeMarco, Barns, and the others were tired, while the skilled samurai still swung their long, razor-sharp weapons with fresh energy.

Then Frank saw the huge samurai leader knock DeMarco to the floor. DeMarco lost his sword, and the samurai raised his curved blade high overhead with both hands.

"Here!" Frank shouted as he leaped onto a bench. Gosaki spun around, and Frank delivered three powerful strikes to his weapon, knocking him over a bench and into a locker.

Frank leaped forward, and with a perfectly controlled thrust brought his weapon's point to the samurai's neck, the sharp tip pricking his throat. Gosaki looked up into Frank's face a moment, then slowly opened his fingers and let his sword drop.

"Do it," the samurai leader snarled as he glared fiercely at Frank. "You have won fairly. I die with honor."

Frank stared down at his opponent, his rapier blade resting against the big man's neck. "No," Frank said. "We both know I won. To kill you like this would be shameful to me."

Frank pulled his blade back from the other's throat.

The samurai stared up at Frank for several moments. Then he slowly rose.

Gosaki faced his fellow samurai. "Finished," he bellowed. The others stopped and looked at him uncertainly.

"This young fighter understands honor," the samurai continued. "To honor *him,* we will fight no more." He turned, and, his eyes straight ahead and his head held high, he moved with dignity toward the door. His men followed him out.

Moments later Joe and Coach Kupcek charged into the room, breathless.

"Frank—where are they? Are you guys okay?" Joe asked.

"We're fine, Joe. It's over. They're leaving."

"Sorry, but we got here as fast as we could," Joe said.

"I know," Frank said. "Thanks for the bailout."

"You're welcome," Joe said. "But next time you decide to leave town like that, I want you to write a note. No mystery phone calls, no strange disappearances, none of this dueling-to-the-death stuff."

"Yes, Mother," Frank said.

"Speaking of Mom," Joe said, "let's go give her a call. I promised I'd tell her where you were as soon as I figured it out myself."

Eau Claire District Library

Frank and Joe's next case:

Frank and Joe witness a daredevil stunt smack in the middle of New York City. A group of parasailors leap off a skyscraper, and one of them ends up crashing to his death. When the Hardys investigate, they discover that the fall was no accident. Murder is on the fly in Manhattan, and when crime flies, no one has a good time. Another series of jumps is in the works, and big money is at stake. So are lives. The Hardys will have to take some heavy-duty leaps of their own to catch the culprits and bring them down for good . . . in *The Last Leap,* Case #118 in The Hardy Boys Casefiles™.

For orders other than by individual consumers, Pocket Books grants a discount on the purchase of **10 or more** copies of single titles for special markets or premium use. For further details, please write to the Vice-President of Special Markets, Pocket Books, 1633 Broadway, New York, NY 10019-6785, 8th Floor.

For information on how individual consumers can place orders, please write to Mail Order Department, Simon & Schuster Inc., 200 Old Tappan Road, Old Tappan, NJ 07675.